LIME AND PUNISHMENT

A NORA BLACK MIDLIFE PSYCHIC MYSTERY

RENEE GEORGE

BARKSIDE OF THE MOON PRESS

Lime and Punishment

A Nora Black Midlife Psychic Mystery Book 11

Publisher: Barkside of the Moon Press

Print ISBN: 978-1-947177-56-7

ACKNOWLEDGMENTS

I have to thank sooo many people for this series!

First, I want to thank my critique partners, Robbin Clubb and Robyn Peterman, for tirelessly reviewing every chapter as I wrote the book and giving me so much feedback. This book is amazing because of them!

Second, to the readers and my Rebels, what would be the point without you all? I am so happy and blessed to have you guys in my corner!

Third, but not least, coffee. Thank you, strong black coffee, for once again being there for me through every step of the writing process. You are a wonderful gift to me and humanity.

For Robbin and Robyn, my Gilly and Pippa. I love you both to the moon.

When Nora is tasked with judging a pie-baking contest, one of the contestants is left pucker-faced when she dies under mysterious circumstances.

My name is Nora Black, and at fifty-seven, I've learned that life—like key lime pie—is equal parts sweet and tart. Business is booming, my best friends are living their best lives, and I am in a great place in my own relationship. In other words, I've never been happier.

Things are finally settling down after that whole murder-on-the-high-seas business, and I haven't been asked to help on a single police investigation for over a year...that is, until I agree to judge the brand-new annual Key Lime Pie Baking Contest.

Big mistake. Huge. When a contestant ends up more than just pucker-faced by keeling over after the contest ends, my no-murder streak curdles fast.

Is it an accident? Or did someone stir up a recipe for *fresh-squeezed murder*?

My psychic nose is whipping up memories that

are equal parts sweet, sour, and deadly, and I'll have to sniff out a killer before someone else gets served up cold.

CHAPTER
ONE

The last bottle of key lime lotion slid into place on the shelf, and I stepped back to admire the row with probably more satisfaction than was actually warranted. Seven years of running Scents & Scentsability, and I still got a little thrill out of a fully stocked display. Business had been steady all week, and the weekend promised to be even better. The Key Lime Festival had kicked off on Monday, and we'd been enjoying an influx of locals and tourists as a result. The finale of the festival was a pie-baking and pie-eating contest that included trophies and money as prizes.

The town mayor, Allison Green, had come up with the festival to generate more tourism revenue for Garden Cove. I was sure it was also some kind of campaign strategy for the next mayoral election, but who cared? Key lime pies were genuinely delicious, tourism was up, and the festival had given me an excuse to develop a key lime soap and lotion that had been flying off the shelves since March.

My partner, Pippa Hines, had gone home early. Her husband, Jordy, was celebrating his twentieth year of sobriety tonight, and Pippa wanted to be there for the milestone. I was in awe of Jordy's commitment to staying clean, and while on paper he and Pippa were opposites, anyone who saw them together would see they were two halves of a whole. I'd known Pippa for a lot of years before she moved to Garden Cove to help me open my shop, and I'd never seen her as happy as she was when she was with Jordy and their children.

I'd found love in Garden Cove as well. Ezra Holden, a GCPD detective, had become a fixture in my life and in my heart. After seven years together, I couldn't imagine a better partner. He'd stayed over last night, and he'd made me coffee and eggs for breakfast. The soft-serve scramble had made me ridiculously giddy.

As I moved behind the sample counter and straightened a row of testers that didn't really need straightening, I thought about the way he'd kissed me goodbye. It had been a promise for later that I fully planned on him making good. Ezra was taking me out tonight to a new Mexican restaurant that had opened in town. Tacos and my hot man were a perfect way to finish the day and start the night.

I was whistling Queen's "I Want to Break Free" as I moved to the front window to flip the closed sign, but an argument outside on the sidewalk stopped me short.

Two women, out on the sidewalk, their voices carrying through the glass with the loud hush of an argument trying to stay polite but failing. I recognized one of them immediately. Leila Rafferty, my ex-husband's wife, and surprisingly, a good friend of mine. Her voice was warm and a little husky. I wasn't sure who she was talking to, but both of them sounded on the verge of escalating.

I looked out the window. Leila stood on the sidewalk in a pale blue linen blouse, her blonde hair loose around her shoulders. It was thick and full and completely her own again after several years in complete remission. I was so happy she'd kicked cancer's butt. My mom had lost her war against the disease eight years ago, and there were parts of me that still grieved when I thought about her. Looking at Leila now, beautiful and healthy, you'd never know the toll radiation and chemotherapy had taken on her.

And now I recognized the woman she was fighting with. Melissa Jones, Edgar Jones's, the bank manager's wife. I'd met Melissa after Edgar had been injured by an exploding popcorn kettle. I'd stayed with him, holding pressure on his wound, until help could arrive. Melissa had brought me fresh-baked bread as a thank-you for saving her husband. Honestly, his injury had been minor, but I hadn't pointed it out. The bread had been delicious.

Melissa was holding herself very straight, the way people do when they're furious and trying not to show it, and her voice, even muffled by the glass, was clipped and harsh.

I hesitated to intervene. It wasn't my business.

Melissa's voice rose a notch as she advanced on Leila, her index finger perilously close to poking Leila's chest. Leila stumbled, and her shoulder hit the window.

It was my business now.

I pushed open the front door.

I stepped out onto the sidewalk and both women turned to look at me.

"Hey," I said, keeping my voice easy, like I'd just

happened to wander out and hadn't witnessed their pissing match. "Everything okay out here?"

It was not. That was obvious. Melissa wore the expression of a woman who'd been told something she clearly didn't want to hear. Leila, on the other hand, looked frustrated and angry.

"We're fine," Melissa said through gritted teeth behind a tight but polite smile.

Leila shook her head, disputing Melissa's assertion. "We're having a disagreement about the judging panel." She pointed to the banker's wife. "Melissa volunteered to be a judge for the pie contest tomorrow, and I had to explain that since her niece has entered the contest means she can't be a judge." She gave an exasperated sigh. "Which I told her last week."

Melissa's jaw tightened. "And I told Leila that I am perfectly capable of judging fairly, regardless of who's in the competition. I've known almost all the contestants my whole life. My niece is one baker among many people who I know and love."

"And I told Melissa," Leila said, "that it's not a question of her integrity. It's a question of the appearance of it."

They both stopped glaring at each other and turned their gazes on me as if I was the deciding vote. I was not. However, I'd worked in the corporate world long enough to know how to mediate a deal.

"Is your niece a good baker?" I asked Melissa.

She blinked, apparently not expecting the question. "She's an excellent baker."

I nodded. "Does she have a real shot at winning?"

"Absolutely." A flash of pride broke through her indignation. "She's been perfecting her recipe for six months."

I nodded. "Then do her a favor and let her win in a way nobody can argue with. It's not your integrity that's in question, Melissa. But if she wins, even if her pie is legitimately the best one there, there will always be people who will wonder if she won on her own merit or if her aunt rigged the competition in her favor. Is that what you want?" I paused. "To taint her victory."

"That's my worry, too," Leila added, when Melissa didn't respond. She lightly rested her hand on the disgruntled woman's arm. "I know you can be impartial, but Gerry would always have this hanging over her head if she were to win. You don't want that on your conscience, do you?"

Melissa's shoulders dropped down a half inch. She looked at Leila for a moment, then away, toward the street, before letting out a long breath. "All right," she said. "I can see your point." She met Leila's eyes. "I officially withdraw."

Leila's relief was visible. "That's really big of you. Thank you, Melissa."

Melissa gave a stiff nod, then turned and walked back up the sidewalk with her dignity intact, which seemed to be what she'd wanted most.

When she was far enough away, Leila, her voice hushed, said, "Girl, thank you. That woman is a handful."

I chuckled. "Happy to be of service."

She arched her brow at me. "Yeah?"

Uh oh. "I mean—"

"Nope, you already said it. You're happy to be of service, and I need servicing."

I laughed again. "Does Shawn know you need servicing?" Leila blushed, and I grinned. "If I didn't have a date tonight, I might..." I raised my hands and shrugged.

She smacked me on the arm, completely deserved. "Stop it," she said on a snort. "That's not the kind of service I require."

I rubbed my forearm where she'd barely made contact, for dramatic effect. "That's a relief. I'd hate to have to cancel my plans on short notice."

"There is something I need from you, though," Leila said.

I groaned and opened the door to the shop. "Come on in, then, while I finish closing up."

Leila followed me inside. The corner of her mouth twitched. "I just have the tiniest of favors to ask."

"How come it doesn't feel tiny?"

She spread her hands out in front of her. "As you know, I just lost a judge for the Key Lime Pie Festival." She tilted her head. "I have two other judges, but I need a third for the tiebreaker."

"No," I said bluntly.

She frowned, her lower lip jutting out in a slight pout.

I gave her a look. "Does that work on Shawn?"

A slow, crooked smile crested her lips. "Usually."

"I guess it's a good thing I'm immune to it."

Leila put her hands together. "Help me, Nora Black-Kenobi. You're my only hope."

"Okay, Princess Leila." The Star Wars reference was a nice touch. I was a bit of a nerd for the franchise. "Why don't you get Shawn to do it?" My ex-husband was the chief of police in our small town. He'd taken over after my dad, the chief before him, had died almost eighteen years ago.

She sighed, letting out a loud, exasperated breath. "He has to do the dog and pony show with the mayor tomorrow." Her eyes were pleading. It made it impossible to tell her no again.

"Fine." I grimaced. "What's involved?"

"Two hours tomorrow afternoon from noon until two on the square. You get to eat a lot of pie...which, I know, terrible," she said with obvious sarcasm, "and then you rank them from first to worst. At the end, you get to crown the winner King or Queen of Key Lime. Plus a pretty substantial cash prize."

I knew they'd been selling tickets for a fifty-fifty drawing for the past several weeks. It was a way to raise funds, where the person who won the ticket draw won half the money, and the other half went to whatever the money was being raised for. I even bought a ticket for myself earlier in the week. "How much is substantial?"

"We've already sold over six thousand dollars' worth of tickets, and Mayor Green has pledged to match the half that goes to the prize baker."

"Wow." I blinked. "That's a lot of dough for one pie."

"Ba-dum-bum." Leila mimicked the joke punchline drum. "Don't quit your day job."

"I thought it was punny." I smirked. "So, that's it. I judge, someone wins, and I'm done."

"Not exactly. After that, there's a key lime pie-eating contest."

"And the winner gets a belly ache?"

Leila snickered. "That and five hundred dollars' worth of gift cards to spend at different businesses around town."

"That's a generous prize for eating pie." I narrowed my gaze at her. "How come you didn't ask me for a donation?"

"I did." She laughed. "Well, I asked Pippa. You weren't here when I was going around to all the stores. She donated a thirty-dollar gift certificate."

I gave Leila a sheepish look. "Oh. Yeah, I think I remember her telling me something about that last month."

"So you'll do it?"

It seemed like one more thing I didn't need to add to my plate. Literally. "Only two hours?" I asked as I mulled it over.

"Give or take."

"And pie."

"An unreasonable amount of pie." She grinned at me with the confidence of someone who already knew the answer.

"Fine," I said. "I'll be your judge."

She threw her arms around me and planted a blustery kiss on my cheek. "You are the absolute best."

"Don't let that get around." I wiped the wet spot on my cheek with the back of my hand. "I have a reputation for being just okay."

"Hah, right. As if." She stepped back, giving my shoulder a pat. "I better get going."

After she left, I flipped the sign to Closed and got my keys.

I'd have to let Pippa know she'd be manning the shop solo for a little while tomorrow. It would be fine. Even if we were busy, I wouldn't be gone for very long, and being a judge meant more exposure for the shop. Free publicity was Pippa's favorite kind of marketing.

A couple of hours. Some tasty pies. Community goodwill. What could go wrong?

A lot, it turns out.

CHAPTER TWO

That evening, Ezra picked me up for our dinner date and took me to a restaurant called Tres Mujeres. It had only been open for a week, but was already a huge hit with the town. Every table was full, and there was a waiting list for seating. The turnover wasn't bad, though, and after fifteen minutes, Ezra and I were seated at a high-top table for two and scanning the menus.

Tres Mujeres had warm terracotta walls decorated with colorful hand-painted tiles in blue, pink, purple, yellow, and green. There were string lights looped across the ceiling and a bar along the back wall lined with every variety of tequila I'd ever heard of and several I hadn't. The whole place smelled like cumin and charred peppers, and traditional mariachi music was being piped through the sound system. Loud enough to feel festive, but not so loud that customers had to shout.

Garden Cove had needed a sit-down Mexican restaurant for years. Don't get me wrong, I still loved the Taco Shake Shack out on Route 9. It had been a staple of the Garden Cove experience dating back to the fifties when my parents had been teenagers. Plus, they made some seriously delicious fried tacos that I had absolutely no intention of giving up. Even so, it was nice to have a place that had some ambience while still serving my favorite kind of food.

Our table was tucked near the window not far from the door. There was a tealight candle glowing in a small clay pot between us and a small vase holding three vibrant orange marigolds. The hostess, and one of the owners, Bernice Lopez, seated us with menus before our server, a young man named Ernesto, brought us a warm basket of chips, two small empty bowls, a carafe of red salsa, and took our drink order. Whoever the first person was who came up with the idea of endless free chips and salsa, in my opinion, deserved all the awards.

Ezra stared at me from across the table, his gaze full of admiration. "You look beautiful." His green eyes caught the candlelight and glinted like emeralds. "If I haven't said it already."

I'd worn a pale lavender dipped-waist midi dress by a young designer out of Kansas City. Too dressy for work, but perfect for date night. Ezra had made sure to tell me how beautiful I looked the moment he'd picked me up at my house. He'd punctuated the compliment with a kiss that had curled my toes.

"You have," I acknowledged with a smile, thinking about that kiss. "But I don't mind hearing it again."

He gave me a knowing nod. "Well, it bears repeating." Ezra's sandy blond hair had gotten a little longer than he usually kept it, long enough to curl slightly at the ears. It made him look almost boyish, even at forty. He wore a sage green sweater that pulled tight across his broad chest and a pair of jeans that hugged his thighs.

He looked almost unfairly good.

"You clean up real nice yourself," I told him. I reached across and stole a chip from his side of the basket.

Ernesto interrupted our mutual admiration club meeting when he returned with our drinks. He set a Dos Equis beer with a lime wedge in front of Ezra and an iced tea in front of me. "Are you ready to order?" he asked.

The place was busy, and I didn't want our dinner getting lost in the wash, so I quickly scanned the taco menu. "I'll take two carnitas tacos and one chicken al pastor."

"Muy bueno," Ernesto said. "Corn or flour tortilla?"

"Corn, definitely," I told him.

He turned to Ezra. "And for you?"

"The enchiladas supreme, but can I exchange the chicken enchilada for another cheese one?"

"Sí," Ernesto said, jotting down the order. "Anything else?"

Ezra raised his brow at me and I shook my head. "That's it for now," he told him. "Thanks, Ernesto."

When the young man left our table, I rubbed my hands together excitedly. "I love tacos almost as much as I love you, so tonight is really working out for me."

He smiled. "High praise indeed."

"The highest."

The candle between us flickered every time the front door opened, which was often. I liked people watching, so I didn't mind being this close to the action…until the front door opened and Melissa and Edgar Jones walked in.

I saw her before she saw me, and I made the immediate and deliberate choice to find the candle flame very interesting.

"Something wrong?" Ezra said.

I put my hand to the side of my face and kept my eyes on the candle. "Nope. Nothing," I lied.

Ezra reached across and put his hand over the one I had resting on the table. "Do you want to leave?"

"No, nothing like that." I dropped my hand from my face and picked up my iced tea and took a sip. Quietly, I said, "Someone just walked in that I would like to avoid if possible."

"Who?" He looked around.

"Stop that," I told him. "I don't want to draw attention."

He leaned forward until his face took on an eerie glow from the candlelight. "What's going on, Nora?"

I grimaced. "I'm avoiding Melissa Jones."

He cast a sideways glance toward the banker and his wife then back to me. "Why?"

"Because." I leaned in and told him about the confrontation between Leila and Melissa, and how Leila had roped me into being a judge for the pie-baking contest after. By the time I'd finished, I'd eaten nearly the whole basket of chips and my salsa bowl was empty.

"Happy coincidence. I'm coordinating security for the baking contest tomorrow." He dropped the lime in his beer and took a swig. "That means I'll get to see you."

"Cute," I said, meaning it. "But you can see why I'd like to avoid Melissa."

"Sounds intense."

"Yep."

He glanced over at Melissa and Edgar. His eyes widened slightly, and he waved. "She's seen you."

I groaned. "I told you not to look," I muttered.

I closed my eyes briefly. When I opened them, I turned just enough to confirm what I already knew. Melissa was standing near the host stand with Edgar, not so much waving as motioning me to come over.

I waved back, smiling pleasantly, but didn't get up.

She started to walk in our direction.

I held up my hand, gesturing for her to wait there for me, then turned back to Ezra. "I'll be right back," I told him. If I let Melissa come to our table, I had no control over how long she stayed. If I went to her, I could decide when I left.

"Take your time." He picked up his drink. "If you need a rescue, give me a signal."

I flashed him a grin. "I'll scream," I said. "Or is that too obvious?"

He chuckled, the corners of his eyes crinkling, and dang if he wasn't so cute that it made Melissa's timing genuinely annoying. I wasn't looking to add any drama to my evening. I was on a date with my hot man, and I had tacos coming.

I left the table and made my way to Melissa.

When Edgar saw me coming, his face went full sunshine. He was a trim man in his late fifties with silver hair. "Nora," he said warmly, taking my hand in both of his. "It is so good to see you."

"You too, Edgar. You're looking well."

"Thanks to you," he said, with total sincerity.

Despite what he told anyone who would listen, I had not saved Edgar Jones's life. I stayed with him after shrapnel from an exploding popcorn kettle had hit him in the shoulder. He'd had to have minor outpatient surgery to repair the wound, but he'd never been in any real danger of dying. At the time of the incident, though, he had initially thought he'd been shot, and we believed a gunman was on the loose. The piece of metal lodged in the gash had kept it from bleeding, so I'd focused on keeping him still and quiet as I'd called 9-1-1 and stayed with him until the paramedics arrived.

"It was nothing," I said.

"You stayed," he asserted. "That's not nothing."

I waved off his praise but nodded my acknowledgement. It had been terrifying, and I hadn't run away and left him alone. I had gotten him help. He was correct. That wasn't nothing. "Thank you."

Melissa cut in before Edgar could heap any more praise on me. "I heard you're going to be taking my spot as a judge for the contest tomorrow."

I winced. "Only as a favor to Leila."

The woman smiled, but it was more feral than friendly. "I'm glad it's you," she said like she wasn't glad at all. "I know I can count on you to give Gerry a fair chance."

Actually, Melissa hardly knew me at all, but I let that point slide. "Is there a reason I wouldn't?"

"Well, you know." Melissa shrugged with too much effort to be nonchalant. "Gerry's soon-to-be ex-husband Bash is Mayor Green's son."

Okay, so this was a surprise. People think that when you live in a small town you know everyone, but it's not true. I knew a good amount of people in my extended circle of friends and customers, and while I sort of remembered that Allison Green had a son and a daughter, I wouldn't have been able to pick either one of them out of a lineup. As for Melissa's niece Gerry, it was the same.

Melissa continued her reasons she thought her niece would be unfairly judged. "I don't trust Rob Doyle or Lance Crabtree as far as I can throw them. I wouldn't put it past them to tank Gerry's chances as a favor to the mayor."

"Doyle and Crabtree?" Rob Doyle was on the town council, and Lance Crabtree was a prosecuting attorney with the DA's office. "Are they judging the bake-off too?"

Melissa nodded. "It's why I wanted to be on the panel." She reached out and squeezed my hand. "Gerry's had a really rough time this past year. What with Bash cheating on her with his secretary." She scoffed. "Talk about a walking cliché." She glanced over her shoulder at her husband. "Edgar would be six feet under if I ever caught him doing something like that."

Edgar looked neither surprised nor angry at her comment. Instead, he looked like a man completely smitten with his wife. He gave her a loving smile and said, "A man would have to be crazy to eat hamburger when he has filet mignon at home."

I managed to stop myself from saying "ew," because comparing his wife to beef was weird and kind of yucky, but also, in its own way, sweet.

Gerry, Melissa told me, was a single mom now with a seven-year-old daughter. She'd worked in catering for a decade and had spent the last two years building a business plan for her own bakery. She was looking at a space on Birch Street, and she'd been developing her key lime pie recipe since January. The prize money would go straight toward her business license and first month's equipment rental.

It didn't take a brainiac to know what Melissa was doing, and I didn't blame her for it. She cared about her niece, and she wanted me to care. I admired it, genuinely. But I wasn't going to judge tomorrow's contest based on a sad backstory.

"Melissa," I said, keeping my voice kind but firm, "I hope Gerry has the best pie there. I really do. But if she wins, it has to be because her pie is the best one on the table. That's the only thing I can judge on." I held her gaze. "You understand."

Something flickered across her face. Disappointment, maybe. But she nodded. "I know. I wouldn't expect anything else."

"I'm rooting for her," I said honestly. "Now, if you'll excuse me—"

I started to turn, and Melissa's hand caught my arm. Not hostile, but urgent. She leaned in before I could step back, and I caught a smell that clung to the sleeve of her blouse, citrusy but not quite lime. Sharper. Floral underneath.

Two women stand in a bright kitchen. Faces blurred, the way they always are in my visions. One of them I know from her voice, along with the blue blouse and the silver earrings. Melissa. She's standing at a counter, and across from her is another woman. Her brown hair is pulled back in a ponytail, jeans and a t-shirt, average build, shorter than Melissa. She's leaning against the counter, her arms folded across her chest.

"I won't be judging anymore," Melissa says. "Leila Rafferty removed me from the panel."

"It doesn't matter." She walks over the center island. "I'm not worried about that." A pause. She keeps her focus on what she's making. "I'm worried about what happens if he doesn't show up."

Melissa reaches across the counter and picks up a clear bottle filled with yellow liquid. "He will." She sounds certain. "Don't worry about him." She tilts the bottle over a measuring spoon, and some of the liquid spills over the rim, catching on her sleeve. She doesn't notice. The smell sharpens. Citrus and flowers. I recognize the scent now. It's yuzu. "After this weekend," Melissa says scathingly, "you won't have to worry about him ever again."

I blinked, staggering a little as the vision ended. Melissa stared at me with concern.

"Are you okay?" Melissa asked.

"Yeah, sure. Sorry," I said, recovering my wits. "It's been a long day. Just zoned out for a second." I extracted my arm gently. "I really hope Gerry has the best pie tomorrow."

I walked back to our table before she could say anything else.

The tacos had arrived during the encounter with Melissa, and I was glad for the happy distraction from the strange vision. Three corn tortilla street tacos on a wooden board, the carnitas pork crisped at the edges and garnished with salsa verde, pickled red onions, and cilantro, and the al pastor topped with cilantro and charred pineapple.

Ezra had waited for me before digging into his own plate of enchiladas, and he'd had our chip basket refilled and our salsa bowls topped off.

I smiled, my mouth watering like Pavlov's dog. "I love you. You know that, right?"

His lips tugged up into a sexy grin. "I know."

I shook my head and picked up the first carnitas taco, folded it, and took a bite. The pork was tender and salty with a little char, and the salsa verde had a zesty kick that was sheer heaven.

So, so good.

Ezra watched me. "Happy?"

I held up one finger, chewed, swallowed. "Very."

He laughed quietly and picked up his own fork.

I took another bite and let the warm noise of the restaurant settle around me. The vision nagged at the edge of my attention. The blurred faces, the unknown woman, probably Gerry, the niece, and the particular dread in her voice when she said *if he doesn't show up*. I'd been getting better at blocking the visions, at building a kind of low wall between myself and whatever emotional static other people carried around with them. But the ones with emotions like fear, anger, and passion behind them still got through. Strong feelings attached to scents made for a tenacious aroma mojo. Or, as Gilly called it, my smell-o-vision. I also couldn't dwell on the psychic moment if I wanted to enjoy my date.

I set the half-eaten taco down and pivoted my gaze to meet Ezra's. "Tell me about your day," I said. "I want to hear all about it."

CHAPTER THREE

Saturday morning, Ezra had left before six. I'd heard him moving around in the dark, waking me up long enough to kiss him goodbye. He had a full day ahead. Coordinating security for the festival was apparently more involved than it sounded, which, knowing Garden Cove, I should have assumed.

By the time I'd gotten up, showered, and wandered next door to Gilly's with my hair still damp, I was feeling pleasantly rested and only mildly apprehensive about judging the pie contest.

Gilly's kitchen smelled like coffee, toast, and the homemade strawberry jam she'd canned the year before. My BFF had gone to a strawberry farm with her husband Scott the previous summer, and she'd come home with a five-gallon bucket of strawberries and a plan. I may have called her Laura Ingalls Wilder a few times and asked her if she was going to be churning butter next.

The joke was on me, because she'd made the most delicious jam ever, and she'd also made me homemade whipped butter to go with it. Not with a churn, mind you. She put heavy whipping cream in a blender, and in less than ten minutes, it had turned into butter and whey.

I was on my second cup of coffee, lots of vanilla cream, and my third piece of toast and jam.

"So," Gilly said, wrapping both hands around her mug. "Tell me about dinner."

I told her about Tres Mujeres, the terracotta walls, the mariachi, the carnitas tacos that had genuinely changed my life, and then about the Joneses walking in, and Melissa taking my attention away from my hot man and the rest of my chips. "I tried to hide from the woman, but it didn't work."

"Why were you avoiding Melissa?"

"Oh, right..." I hadn't told her about the pie contest thing yet. "Leila and Melissa were arguing outside the shop yesterday. Leila was trying to remove Melissa as a judge because her niece entered the contest, and it's a conflict of interest."

"And you got involved?" She made it a question.

"Yes." I groaned. "Leila seemed like she needed help." I waved off whatever she was going to say next. "Anyways, I stepped in, like the superhero I am, and saved the day."

Gilly smirked. "And..."

"And then Leila asked me to take Melissa's place on the judging panel, and I said yes."

"Just like that?" My BFF tucked her chin and scoffed. "You can't even boil water. How are you qualified?"

I waved my strawberry jam toast at her and said, "Those who can't do, judge. Besides, my cooking skills might be bad, but my tastebuds are highly attuned."

She shook her head. "I still can't believe you said yes," she added. "It's so off brand." Her expression and tone were teasing.

"Hey, I can be civic minded." I finished my bite and washed it down with a sip of coffee. "Besides, I really like pie. And I couldn't say no to Leila."

Gilly arched her well-shaped eyebrow at me. "You couldn't, huh?"

"She made a Star Wars reference and pouted."

"That would make it hard to say no." My BFF snorted. "Leila doesn't strike me as a sci-fi nerd."

"She's not!" I threw up my hands. "Which is why I had to reward her efforts."

"Okay, back to dinner. What happened when you ran into Melissa on your date?"

I filled her in quickly, Gilly listening with her full attention. When I got to the part about Melissa lobbying me to look out for Gerry, she made a soft sound in her throat. "She means well."

"I know, but jeez. She was blatantly transparent about it."

"Gerry's had a rough year." Gilly set her mug down. "You know who her ex is, right?"

"I didn't until Melissa told me. Bash Green, Mayor Green's son, apparently."

"Yep. He works for his father's real estate business." Her tone was wry. "From what I've been told, he shows up occasionally and cashes a check."

"Nepotism at its worst."

"One hundred percent." She picked up her toast, put it back down without eating any. "He's always had a reputation. A real player. Charming, good-looking, completely unreliable. I genuinely thought he'd turned a corner when he married Gerry. She seemed to steady him, and folks talked a lot less about him." A pause. "I was wrong, apparently."

"His secretary," I said.

Gilly's expression did the rest. Then, quietly, she said, "Their poor daughter."

I knew her thoughts were no longer on Gerry's daughter, but on her own children. Gio Rossi had taken a job as a head chef in Vegas when they were married, and he'd gone without Gilly and the kids, with the excuse that he would move them out after he got settled. Instead, he'd cheated on Gilly. Ari and Marco had been seven at the time. Explaining to her children why their father had abandoned his family hadn't been on her Crap Things That Happen Bingo Card. She'd softened the blow as much as she could, and Gio had come out of the deal virtually unscathed. Gilly was a major catch, which shows what an idiot Gio Rossi was. The man should count himself lucky I hadn't been around at the time, because...well, there was a lot of desert in Nevada for a body to disappear.

"Divorce is always hard on the kids," she said.

"It is."

She picked up her mug and took a sip. "Did Melissa say anything else?"

"Not really, but I did have a vision."

Gilly's gaze snapped to mine. "Way to bury the lead." She scooted toward me. "Give me all the deets."

"When I tried to get back to my table, Melissa grabbed my arm. She'd spilled yuzu juice on her sleeve, and the sharp citrus scent took me in." I walked her through the vision. The woman I was fairly certain was Gerry working in a kitchen with Melissa. They were making pies and talking about some guy Gerry was worried about. "She said, 'I'm worried about what happens if he doesn't show up,' and Melissa replied, 'After this weekend, you won't have to worry about him ever again.'"

Eyes wide now, Gilly asked, "What does that even mean?"

"Your guess is as good as mine."

"They were talking about Bash, right?"

"I don't know. They didn't mention any names."

Gilly was quiet for a moment. "If it was Gerry, it has to be Bash."

"That's where my head went."

"Do you think he's in danger?" She shook her head. "Melissa saying she won't ever have to worry about him again sounds pretty threatening."

"I know." I turned my mug in a slow circle on the table. "But killing him or whatever seems pretty extreme. Even for Melissa. 'After this weekend' could just mean after Gerry wins, she'll have some money for a fresh start." I paused. Even if the prize was six thousand or more dollars, it wasn't "starting over" money. However... "Maybe she wants the prize money so she can hire a good divorce attorney."

Gilly gave me a look that said she also thought probably, but who knows. We'd investigated enough murders over the past eight years not to have alternative and more nefarious scenarios running around in our heads.

"Probably better not to nose around," she said, and then caught herself and laughed. "Poor choice of words. Unintentionally punny."

I rolled my eyes. "I have no interest in getting involved in a domestic dispute."

"Oh, and Melissa was certain the other judges were in Green's pocket," I said, because it had been sitting at the back of my mind since Melissa mentioned them the night before. "Rob Doyle and Lance Crabtree. You know them?"

Gilly dried her hands on the dish towel. "I know Rob. Town council." She paused. "He's a jerk."

I knew Rob and didn't disagree. "Even so, I'm not sure if he would rig a pie-baking contest."

Gilly nodded. "He's not a criminal. He's just—" She searched for it. "Smug. The kind of man who thinks his opinion improves whatever room he walks into." She folded a tea towel over the oven handle. "Lance, I don't know as well. He seems like a nice guy. His grandfather is a retired judge." She tapped her chin. "I can't see either of them tanking a baking contest to curry favor with Allison Green. That's a lot of risk for very little reward."

"That's what I figured." I sighed. "Melissa has her guard up when it comes to her niece. She is probably seeing zebras in a herd of horses."

"Probably," Gilly agreed.

I pushed back from the center island and carried my mug to the sink. I was tired of talking about Melissa Jones, so I changed the subject to something we both loved. "How's Ari liking NASA?"

"Why did you have to remind me that my baby is halfway across the country?" She whined, but she was smiling.

"Sorry," I said. Not sorry at all. Gilly, as she should be, was so proud of Ari. The girl had excelled in high school and college, graduating early from Sanderson Institute of Technology. She had been courted by several multibillion-dollar tech corporations, but in the end took the more modest offer from NASA as a cybersecurity specialist.

"I honestly don't know where she gets her

brains," Gilly said. "It certainly wasn't from Gio or me."

"Well." I leaned against the counter. "Definitely not Gio."

She laughed, short and sharp. "Accurate." She reached past me to put the jam in the fridge. "Marco's coming home for the summer, at least. I'm looking forward to that."

But something in the way she said it made me wonder if there was more she wasn't saying. I watched her face. She was still smiling, but the edges of her eyes had gone tight.

"Give," I said. "What's going on?"

"Nothing." She closed the fridge. "Probably nothing."

"Gilly."

She crossed her arms. "I just get a weird feeling. Like something's off with him. Whenever I ask, he tells me we'll talk about stuff when he gets home." She shook her head. "His grades are fine. I have all his account logins because I pay his tuition every month through his dashboard. He's a solid B/C student. So, I don't think it's about school."

Marco played baseball at Central University. He'd been recruited from the community college he'd played at, and they'd given him a scholarship that covered a lot of his college expenses, including his dorm room. He was in his senior year. Marco had always been athletic, handsome, and charming, which meant socially, his life had been pretty good. However, he'd always struggled with academics. If he was maintaining passing grades, it meant he was taking his classes seriously.

"When's the last time you talked?"

"Two weeks ago." She wiped crumbs from the center island. "He texts and calls, but he never really says anything."

I snorted. "That could just be his age. Ezra complains about the same thing with Mason." Mason, who graduated with Marco and Ari, was working on his master's degree at MU.

"Maybe, but it just feels...different." She frowned. "A mom knows."

She said it with such complete certainty that I didn't argue. I was no mother, by choice, and I'd made my peace with that decision a long time ago. Which meant I had exactly zero authority to weigh in on what her instincts about her own kid were or weren't worth.

"Fair enough," I told her. "He'll be home in a few weeks. Try not to worry too much until you can do something about it. Whatever it is, you'll handle it."

She nodded, but her expression said the subject wasn't closed.

We looked at each other.

"We should get to work," I said. "Pippa is already going to be on her own for a bit today. I don't want to wear out her goodwill by being late on top of it. And you have a new business to run."

That got a real smile. "I can't believe my spa area is finally done."

I was seriously happy for Gilly. She had a man who loved her the way she deserved to be loved, and the business she'd always wanted. She was living her dream. "Are you fully booked?"

"Every slot." She beamed with pride. "I've been training Carly and Sarina. They're good. Our schedule is solid with established clients, new referrals, and the oncology slots."

The expansion of Gilly's massage space had been delayed, then resumed, then delayed again between construction problems, permits, and the usual parade of small disasters. It had finally been finished in March, and watching her move through all of it, watching her build something that was hers, had been amazing.

"I'm so proud of you, Gills," I said.

She grabbed her purse as we headed out. "I couldn't have done it without you."

"Yes, you could have." Sure, I'd bought the building, but she had done everything else. I held the back door open. "You basically did."

I drove to work feeling hopeful and optimistic.

Today was going to be an awesome day.

CHAPTER FOUR

The town square was already buzzing when I left Scents & Scentsability at twenty minutes to noon. The dogwoods along the perimeter were in full bloom, white and pink against a blue sky, and the seasonal planters the town put out each spring were bursting with yellow and purple pansies. Tourists and townsfolk moved in loose clusters along the storefronts, shopping bags looped over wrists, coffee cups and fountain drink cups in hand. A few locals I recognized called out greetings as I passed.

"Hey, Nora." Tom Briggs from the hardware store gave me a nod from his doorway.

"Staying busy?" asked Paulette Marsh, who ran the candle shop two doors down from me.

"Always," I told her with a smile.

I heard the square before I fully saw it. The crowd noise carried up the street, getting louder as I rounded the corner to the courthouse lawn.

The grandstand pavilion had been dressed up in green and white. Bunting ran along the front edge of the stage, and someone had gone to considerable trouble with the judging table. It was draped in white linen, studded with small potted lime trees, and green ribbon bows at each corner. On the table itself, arranged on tiered stands of varying heights, sat more pies than I had ever seen assembled in one place outside of a bakery. I counted quickly, lost count, and estimated somewhere north of twenty. Every single one of them was gorgeous. Elaborate meringue peaks, glossy glazed tops, and decorative crusts crimped into unique patterns. The color of the filling ranged from pale chartreuse to a green so vivid it was practically neon. The pies were labeled with numbers, not names.

I stared at the puckeringly sweet smorgasbord in front of me.

Maybe I had bitten off more than I could chew. Literally.

Rob Doyle and Lance Crabtree were already up on the stage when I climbed the steps. Rob was a compact man in his late forties. He looked relaxed and confident.

"Nora Black," he said. "Heard you were stepping in." The way he said it managed to imply both that he approved and that I should be flattered he approved.

Whatever. "Rob." I shook his hand. "Just doing my part."

He laughed as if I'd told the funniest joke.

Lance Crabtree was younger, mid-to-late thirties, with an easy, open face. He had dressed up slightly more than the occasion required, in beige linen pants and a matching jacket. Linen was a cool fabric, but the sun was out, and I had a feeling it was only going to get warmer.

He extended a hand and smiled. "Welcome to the fold, Nora." He glanced at the judging table, and his expression mirrored exactly what I'd felt thirty seconds ago. "I'll be honest, I was not expecting this many pies."

"Neither was I," I said.

"Don't let it intimidate you," Rob said, in a tone that suggested he was not intimidated in the least. "We don't have to eat the whole pie. Just a bite." He chuckled. "Probably."

Down on the courthouse lawn, rows of folding

chairs had filled up steadily, and the grass beyond them was dotted with picnic blankets, personal camp chairs, and the organized chaos of family outings. Coolers were cracked open, children were having their faces painted near the far end, and a man in a yellow vest was twisting balloon animals for a cluster of kids who had strong opinions about the shapes they wanted. A short distance from the judging stage, a second table sat on the grass with ten seats lined up behind it and a stack of white bakery boxes in front of each place. The pie-eating contest, if I had to guess.

On a separate elevated platform to the left of the grandstand, a row of chairs faced the lawn. Mayor Allison Green sat center, composed and camera-ready in a green blazer.

I shook my head. The woman didn't have a subtle bone in her body.

Beside her were Chief of Police Shawn Rafferty, two aldermen I recognized from town council meetings, and a few other official-looking people I couldn't immediately name. A podium with a microphone stood at the front of the platform.

I scanned the perimeter for Ezra. Near the far corner of the lawn, I spotted Officers Reese and Broyles in their department polos, working the crowd line. Reese caught my eye and raised a hand. I waved back. No Ezra yet.

Leila appeared at my elbow, slightly breathless, like she'd been moving fast all morning and hadn't stopped. "Hey," she panted. "You made it."

"Did you have doubts?"

She giggled. "No. Not really."

"What's with the numbers?"

"It was always going to be a blind taste test," she said. "No baker names on the pies."

"Then why not Melissa?"

Leila lifted an eyebrow and gave me an "I know you're not stupid" look. "You're telling me she wouldn't know which pie was Gerry's?"

"Fair point." I nodded. "How much is the prize total now?"

She leaned in and whispered, "Eleven thousand dollars."

"What?" I said too loudly.

Leila patted the air. She glanced toward the mayor's platform and dropped her voice further. "Don't say anything. Green wants to make the announcement."

"I can understand why." I let out a low whistle. "That's a lot of freaking money."

"You have no idea. Between ticket sales and

Green matching the baker's half, I honestly can't believe it." She shook her head. "It's a crazy amount of money for a pie." A beat. "Makes me wish I'd entered."

"Can you bake?"

"I'm not bad." She laughed. "For eleven grand, I'd become an expert."

Mayor Green stepped up to the podium and tapped the microphone. The ambient noise of the square softened. "Welcome, Garden Cove and honored guests," she said with the practiced warmth of someone used to addressing her constituents. She held up her hands, pausing for dramatic effect, then dropped the big news. "This year's fifty-fifty drawing raised a total of eleven thousand dollars."

Around the lawn, heads turned and voices rose in a ripple of surprise. I was pretty sure that if this became an annual festival, next year would see quadruple the number of entries. I would definitely not be judging that one. While I liked pie, I didn't like it that much.

Green continued. "The winner of the ticket drawing will receive five thousand five hundred dollars." Another pause. "And thanks to the generosity of our sponsors and our matching pledge, the winner of today's Key Lime Pie Baking Contest will take home eleven thousand dollars."

There were claps, whistles, and the murmurs turned into a dull roar. Eleven thousand for a pie contest was not a small-town prize. At five dollars a ticket, they'd sold at least twenty-two hundred tickets. That was a lot of people with five dollars, a hope and a prayer. Though I imagined some had bought more than one.

The mayor called for silence again and said, "But wait...there's more." She wiggled her eyebrows and grinned. "We had a lot more entries than we expected, so we're also awarding cash prizes for second and third place — five hundred dollars for second and two hundred fifty for third."

More cheers and applause. Green knew how to work a crowd, no doubt about it.

Leila tapped my arm. "I better go. Have fun." She was already moving.

I turned back to the table to get my bearings, and that's when I heard the argument to the left of the grandstand, near the pie-eating table. Two voices pitched low and urgent in the way of people trying to fight without being seen. I leaned forward and glanced around the obscuring bunting.

A young woman stood with her arms crossed

and her jaw set. She had on high-waisted skinny jeans and an oversized t-shirt knotted at the hip, and her brown hair fell loose over her shoulders. Across from her, a man leaned in with the energy of someone who thought proximity was a form of argument. They both looked to be in their late twenties or early thirties.

"What are you even doing here?" she demanded. "Leave me alone."

"You can't keep me from our daughter." His voice was low and coiled. "I'll go for full custody if you try. I'll take her away from you if you force my hand."

"Now you want to be a father?" She clenched her fists at her sides. "Go away, Bash. I can't do this right now."

Bash.

I looked at her more carefully. Brown hair, average build, shorter than Melissa. The hair was down instead of pulled back, but the color was the same. If that was Bash, this had to be Gerry.

She turned to walk away, then stopped. Something across the lawn had caught her eye, and whatever it was drained the color from her face. She turned sharply back the way she'd come, pushing past Bash and moving quickly in the opposite direction. I followed her sight line, searching the crowd for whatever had spooked her. Faces, strollers, lawn chairs, a man selling lemonade. Nothing I could pick out as unusual.

Bash watched her go. His expression wasn't angry anymore. It was something harder to read.

"Ready?"

I turned. Rob was back on the stage, Lance beside him, both looking at me expectantly. Rob was holding three forks, offering one to each of us.

I took mine.

"Ready," I said.

By the thirteenth pie, I was regretting the three pieces of toast I'd had that morning and my life choices in general. Key lime pie is delicious in small amounts. In large amounts, it was intensely sweet and brutally tart, and no amount of meringue was going to tame it. I couldn't stop my mouth from watering and wondered, more than once, if I was going to drool in front of the hundreds of people gathered on the courthouse lawn.

We had bottles of water to cleanse our palates between tastings, but it was going to take a toothbrush and a tongue scraper to fully reset my mouth. I finally caught sight of Ezra moving through the crowd below and caught his eye. I gave him a look that I hoped conveyed, *slap me if I ever agree to something like this again.*

I ranked the current pie. The scoring scale ran to a maximum of ten points each for taste, presentation, and creativity.

"This one has an artificial taste to it," Rob said. He gave it a two for taste, a five for presentation, and a two for creativity. Ouch.

I couldn't taste anything artificial, but that didn't mean it wasn't there. I gave the pie a six, seven, and six. That seemed fair.

"Are we ready for the next one?" Rob asked. I didn't know why he'd assumed point, but I was glad someone had. The sugar was fogging my brain.

I took a long drink of water, swished it around, and gave him a thumbs up.

Lance snickered. "Only twelve more to go."

I groaned louder than I'd meant to, and both men laughed. The next pie was covered in beautiful meringue rosettes and finished with thin slices of candied lime and a dusting of zest. The custard, a vibrant yellow-green, was set firm and holding its shape. Surprisingly, the baker had mellowed the tartness with vanilla. I could see the tiny dark seeds flecked throughout the custard. I hummed appreciatively on the first bite.

"This one is different," I said.

Lance nodded.

I looked over at Rob. He was frowning as he marked it with a four, five, and a five.

I gave it a nine, nine, and a nine. I couldn't see Lance's scores, but I hoped he was more generous than Rob.

After the next five, I made a mental note to call my GP on Monday and inquire about diabetes testing. They were all fine, but none of them had come close to lucky number thirteen.

Pie number nineteen was decorated with a lattice crust, meringue shaped into leaves along the inside edge, and a custard that leaned almost orange. "Interesting." I brought the fork to my nose first. Brightly citrus, with floral notes underneath. I couldn't be certain this was Gerry's pie, but since nothing else we'd tasted had used the bitter fruit, I thought it probably was.

The crust was buttery and flaky with just enough salt to offset the sweetness. The yuzu gave grapefruit vibes, a hint of bitterness and acidity that enhanced rather than competed with the key lime. I hated to admit it after twenty-five bites of pie, but it was freaking delicious. I gave it tens across the board without hesitation. I looked over at Rob's sheet, and once again, he'd given a great pie, a terrible score. All fours. There was no accounting for taste in some people.

After the twenty-fifth and final pie, I was ready for antacids and a long nap. We handed our score sheets to a young woman who carried them off to be tallied.

"Which was your favorite?" Lance asked.

"Nineteen," I said. "But thirteen was close. Either one deserves to win."

Lance nodded. "I'm a sucker for vanilla and lime, so thirteen got me. Nineteen was excellent, though. I gave it high marks."

We both looked at Rob. He shrugged. "There were a few that rose to the top for me."

I didn't believe him, but I also couldn't figure out why he'd lie about a pie.

"Can we get all the bakers up in front of the grandstand, please?" Mayor Green's voice came over the speakers. "We're about to announce the winners."

Twenty-five people, mostly women and a few men, made their way through the crowd to stand in front of us. The woman I was fairly sure was Gerry was among them.

"I just want to thank every single baker for their efforts today," Green said. "Judging by the scoring, you all did a great job, but three standouts were separated by only a couple of points." She leaned into the mic. "In third place, number thirteen — Sandy Johnson. Congratulations, Sandy!"

A middle-aged blonde waved her hand and shouted, "That's me!"

"Only one point separates first and second place. In second place is number nineteen...my very own daughter-in-law, Geraldine Green. Congratulations, Gerry!"

Green clapped with the crowd, her smile tight and not quite reaching her eyes.

Gerry raised her hand, but she looked like she was going to be sick. As far as I was concerned, she'd been robbed. So had Sandy. Who had taken first? No one else had come close.

"And the winner of the first annual Key Lime Pie Baking Contest, taking home eleven thousand dollars, is..." A drumroll played over the speakers. "Number three...Dora Charles!"

"I won!" A tall redhead threw her hands in the air. "I won!"

I tried to place number three in my memory and landed on a pie buried under a mountain of meringue, baked-Alaska style. It had been good. Not remarkable. But it had come early in the rotation when I'd still been generous with my scores, and I suspected Rob and Lance had done the same. I shook my head. Sandy and Gerry were leaving with seven hundred and fifty dollars between them. It wasn't right.

"Winners, please make your way around the back of the grandstand for photos and instructions for collecting your prize money," Green said. "And can we get our ten pie-eating contestants to the table to the left of the grandstand?"

Eight men and two women moved to the table and stood behind their chairs.

"I'm going to hand things over to our very own Chief of Police, Shawn Rafferty," Green continued, gesturing toward Shawn as he stood. "Let's give Chief Rafferty a big hand."

They shook hands. Green exited the stage. Shawn cleared his throat. "Are we ready to watch some people stuff their faces with pie?"

The crowd was enthusiastic. I was not. After one or two bites of twenty-five different pies, the last thing I wanted was a front-row seat to competitive eating. I stuck around for about ten minutes as Shawn entertained the crowd and announced the contestants, before I'd decided, I done my civic duty for the day. I turned to let Rob and Lance know I was heading out, but both of them were already gone. I was the last rat on this sinking ship, apparently. I hadn't even noticed when they'd left.

I made my way down the steps and around the back of the grandstand where the photo session was setting up. I wanted to congratulate the winners, tell Sandy and Gerry in particular how much I'd loved their pies, and, I supposed, say something gracious to Dora.

"Where's Geraldine Green?" A man with a camera slung around his neck scanned the small group. "We need her for the picture."

"I saw her heading toward the portable toilets," someone said.

After a few minutes, the photographer said, "Can someone go check on Geraldine? Otherwise, we'll have to get the shot without her."

The mayor, who stood at the back, had her hands clasped behind her back in a not-it stance, her gaze fixed somewhere above everyone's heads.

"I'll go," I said.

I crossed the lawn to the row of seven portable

toilets. Three showed occupied. I knocked on the first one.

"Occupied. Can't you read?" A man's voice.

"Sorry." I moved to the next. "Gerry?" I knocked lightly.

"Nope. Brandon, not Gerry," came the reply.

I knocked on the last occupied door. "Gerry?"

"It's busy." I recognized the voice. Lance.

"Sorry, Lance. I'm looking for one of the winners."

"Nora?" His tone was confused. "She's not in here."

Then I heard him retch.

"Sorry," I said quickly, stepping back.

I started opening the unoccupied stalls one by one. When I reached the last one and pulled the door open, I felt the blood drain from my face.

Gerry was slumped on the toilet, crumpled forward, completely still. I reached inside and gave her a light shake. "Gerry?"

Nothing. "I need help!" I shouted toward the crowd. "Someone call 9-1-1!"

I felt for a pulse and couldn't find one. I needed to get her onto the ground to start CPR. I stepped into the stall and the door swung shut behind me.

I tried to ignore the sharp chemical smell of the

toilet sanitizer as I got my arms under Gerry and lifted.

It's dark. There is only a thin trickle of light coming in from a vent near the roof.

"You stupid woman," a voice hisses.

"I didn't know," a woman says. "I thought—"

Bodies hit the plastic walls. Outside, footsteps pass. I can't make out what anyone is saying.

"Shut up before I shut you up for good." A man's voice, I think, though the dark makes everything uncertain.

A whimper. A squeal of pain.

Muttered cursing. Then, harsh and final: "This is your fault. You made me do this."

I came back gasping, the twenty-five key lime pies making a serious bid for freedom. I pulled Gerry with me as I backed out the door into the sunlight, and we both went down onto the grass.

I could see her eyes now. They were red and bloodshot, with tiny red pinpoint spots scattered across the skin around her eyelids. Petechial hemorrhaging. A clear sign of suffocation.

Ezra, Reese, and Broyles were already running across the lawn toward us, shouting. They were too late. It had been too late before I'd found her.

I rolled away from Gerry and was sick in the grass.

Lance came out of his stall and looked at me with sympathy. "You too?"

I shook my head. Ezra reached me then, getting a hand under my arm and pulling me to my feet. "Are you all right?"

"I'm fine," I rasped. I pointed at Gerry on the ground behind me, where Reese and Broyles had already crouched down. "But Gerry Green has been murdered."

CHAPTER FIVE

Ezra helped me to my feet as Reese and Broyles crouched over Gerry on the grass. Reese checked her airway while Broyles started compressions. Ezra stepped away for a moment and called for backup and to check on the status of the paramedics. The crowd noise from the pie-eating contest on the other side of the grandstand continued, oblivious to the horrible situation going on less than a hundred yards away.

That hadn't stopped a small crowd of onlookers from forming near us. They were curious, people asking who had been injured and why were the police doing CPR. I heard one person say, "Must've been a heart attack."

I gave a slight headshake, not directed at

anyone. A heart attack was possible. I'd thought that when I first saw her slumped in the stall. She'd looked stressed out earlier. But her eyes...that was the unmistakable sign of petechial hemorrhaging. That happens when someone is suffocated or choked.

"The paramedics are on their way," Ezra said when he returned to me. "I've called for backup."

Shawn jogged across the field as uniformed officers arrived on the scene. "Get these people back," he instructed them. "Cordon off the area."

"Chief," Ezra greeted him when Shawn reached us.

"Lay out the situation for me," he said.

"Nora discovered Geraldine Green in a portable toilet shortly after the pie-baking contest ended."

Shawn arched his brow at me.

I shrugged, still feeling ill. "They needed her for the publicity shots, and someone said they saw her heading over here. After a few minutes, they asked if someone could check on her. I volunteered."

"Is she...?" He let the question linger as he looked over at Reese and Broyles' efforts.

"Yes," I said. "But not for long, I don't think."

He nodded. It was standard procedure to perform CPR, even if someone seemed dead-dead, if they hadn't been dead for very long. First responders were obligated to try if there was even a slight chance resuscitation might be possible.

Mayor Green was gesturing urgently at Shawn. His lips thinned and his frown deepened. "I'll be back."

I reached out and grabbed his arm before he could leave. He gave me a questioning look.

"Gerry," I pointed to the victim, "is Mayor Green's daughter-in-law."

"I know," Shawn said. "I'll be tactful. Don't worry."

"I'm not worried about that." I shook my head. "Gerry was separated from her husband, Green's son, and they got into a fight before the taste testing. He made some threats against her."

"He threatened to harm her?"

I shook my head. "No. He said he'd fight for full custody of their daughter if she tried to keep her from him. It gives him a motive."

"I'll keep that in mind," Shawn said. He left us and went to meet with the mayor.

Ezra squeezed my shoulder. "This is Melissa Jones's niece, right?"

"Yes." The poor woman.

Two EMS agents, Bob Coleman, the senior paramedic, and a younger woman I didn't recognize, jogged over with a bag and a defibrillator case. The pair immediately took over for Reese and Broyles.

"They were quick," I said to Ezra.

"They were working the festival, so already here," Ezra told me. "Are you feeling better?"

"Still nauseated," I told him. "But barfing the pies up seems to have helped some."

He made a face. "Yuck."

"You're telling me." I shook my head and it felt swimmy. "I'm not sure what was worse, getting all that pie down, or it deciding to come back up." I could still taste the sour bile in my mouth. "Nope," I amended. "Coming back up was definitely worse."

Reese and Broyles stepped aside for the EMTs. Reese's shoulders were slumped, and Broyles put a hand on the back of her neck then slid his fingers down her back in a brief but intimate gesture. Bob took over compressions while his partner slid Gerry's oversized shirt up and applied the pads under her left breast and over the right side of her chest. I held my breath as the AED cycled through its assessment. The robotic voice announced no shockable rhythm detected. They tried again. Same result.

The paramedics kept working anyway. They injected her with something, then tried the machine again. Nothing. Finally, Bob stopped and glanced over at Ezra. He shook his head.

This certainly wasn't my first dead body, and I was far from squeamish. Even so, I staggered a few feet from Ezra and hurled again.

He placed a hand on my back and gripped my shoulder to keep me upright. "Ungh," I moaned through shallow breaths. "I don't want you to see me like this."

Bob came over with a syringe. "Zofran," he explained. "For nausea and vomiting." He gestured toward me. "Do you want it?"

As another wave hit me, I nodded emphatically. "I want."

Bob pushed my sleeve up, wiped my upper arm with an alcohol pad, then injected the medicine into my deltoid. "It's quick acting. You should feel better soon."

I gave him a wan smile. "Thanks, Bob. You're the best."

"Tell my wife that," he joked.

"The next time I see Nana, I will do just that." I'd met Bob's wife at an AA meeting where he was celebrating eighteen years of sobriety. Pippa, Gilly, and I had crashed the public meeting while investigating the death of Dolly Paris. Bob had been warm and welcoming to us, and that was the night Pippa found out her sister Tippi had started her own sobriety journey.

Lance Crabtree stood with the other potential witnesses at the end of the portable toilets, his arms folded and his expensive linen jacket draped over one arm. After he'd come out of the stall, he'd taken one look at Gerry on the grass and gone the color of old chalk. I saw him raise his hand to his mouth a couple of times. I felt his pain.

"I think someone else might need a shot of Zofran," I told Bob, gesturing over at Lance. "He started throwing up before me."

Bob gave a sharp nod. "I'll go assess him."

"Both of you have nausea and vomiting?" Ezra frowned at me. "Do you think one of the pies made you both sick?"

"I think all the pies made me sick," I answered. "But I don't know. Rob ate the same pies we did. I haven't seen him since the judging."

Ezra raised his hand and did a quick wrist flick. Levi Walters, a uniformed officer I'd worked with before, came running over. "I need you to locate Robert Doyle. Do you know who he is?"

"Yes, sir." Levi ran a hand through his dark hair. "Is he a suspect?"

"Not at this time," Ezra told him. "Just want a wellness check. Make sure he's okay."

Jeanna Treece, Levi's partner, was interviewing potential witnesses. I caught pieces of it. One of the men who'd been in the portable toilets at the time said, "I didn't hear anything. I would have heard something."

The anti-nausea medication was starting to take the edge off, helped along considerably by the fact that my stomach was essentially empty. I was shaky and cold despite the afternoon sun, and I had no interest in thinking about pie ever again for the rest of my natural life.

Ezra walked me away from prying ears. "Anything else you want to tell me?" He touched the side of his own nose, briefly, lightly.

I glanced around. Reese and Broyles were familiar with my scratch-and-sniff visions, so I wasn't worried about them. "There's more," I told Ezra. "When I went into the stall to get her out, there was the strong scent of odor control chemicals, and it triggered a memory."

Ezra waited.

"It was dark. Almost no light. Just the vent near the top of the stall. Two people. One of them was Gerry, I think, because I can only suppose one person was attacked in a porta-potty." I paused, trying to retrieve something solid from the dark blur of it. "I think the other was a man. The voice was whispering and harsh, so I can't be certain, but the other person just felt...male. Gerry hit the walls trying to get away." I stopped. "He did something to quiet her. I think that's when he..." I gestured toward the young woman, now covered with a blanket. "He said, 'This is your fault. You made me do this.'"

Ezra was quiet for a moment. "Anything else? Height, clothing, anything?"

"It was too dark. I'm sorry." I wasn't apologizing for the vision's limitations exactly. Ezra knew, after all these years, how the scent memories worked, but chances were good her attacker was close by, and any physical clues would have made all the difference in finding them fast.

He put a hand on my shoulder for a moment, then let it drop as Shawn strode over again. When he reached us, he looked at the covered form on the grass, then at Ezra, then at me. "Situation report," he said to Ezra.

Ezra gave it to him cleanly and without editorializing. "Victim is Geraldine Green, thirty-one years old, one of the contest winners, found unresponsive in the last portable toilet by Nora. Petechial hemorrhaging consistent with suffocation. No shockable rhythm on the AED. Coroner and forensic team are en route. The three people confirmed in the adjacent stalls are being interviewed. No confirmed witnesses to the victim's entry or a suspect's exit."

Shawn turned his gaze on me. "You have anything useful beyond the physical discovery?" His tone was interested, not sarcastic. He'd grown to appreciate my gifts over the years. While Shawn and I had had our differences, hence the reason we weren't married anymore, him trusting me had never been a problem.

I glanced at Ezra, who gave me a barely perceptible nod. "I've had two visions. One yesterday, when I was talking to her aunt. She was in a kitchen, maybe hers, maybe her aunt's, and she was scared of someone. A man. I also had one in the stall when I found her. It was too dark to make out any details. I wish I had more insight, but that's all I have right now."

Shawn ran a hand through his hair. Unhappily, he said, "The mayor wants this resolved quickly and quietly. Minimal press, fast answers."

Of course that's what she wanted. Her estranged daughter-in-law was dead on the courthouse lawn at Allison Green's festival. It was a political nightmare for her.

"I'd like you to consult with Detective Holden and his team, officially," Shawn said. "Your usual compensation. If that's workable for you."

Like he'd have been able to stop me. "Yes. Absolutely. Anything I can do."

Shawn's phone rang and he walked away to take the call. The forensics team arrived, and Reese and Broyles took them over to the portable toilet.

Now that the nausea had abated, I ran what I knew through my head. Someone had killed Gerry Green in a porta-potty at her soon-to-be-ex-mother-in-law's festival, in broad daylight, surrounded by hundreds of people, and walked away without being seen. That took either extraordinary nerve or extraordinary luck. Possibly both.

What I didn't know was whether the "he" from my vision in the stall was the same "he" that had terrified Gerry enough to reverse direction on a crowded lawn. Or even the same "he" she'd hoped, from the kitchen vision, would show up today. She'd been angry with Bash when they'd been fighting by the grandstand, but she'd seemed afraid of him but also resolved. Of course, when it came to domestic violence, that didn't always matter. Men could turn dangerous when their egos and pride got involved. But Bash Green had been standing right behind her when she'd gotten scared of something or someone and turned to push past him. Maybe he'd seen something that could help the police. Then there was Melissa's "after this weekend, you won't have to worry about him ever again" promise. Had she been talking about Bash or someone else?

I heard a peal of children laughing and my gut clenched. It reminded me that there was a seven-year-old girl somewhere in Garden Cove who was going to need someone to explain to her that her mother wasn't coming home.

I had lost my mom as an adult. I'd had fifty-one years of her, and it had still knocked me flat. I couldn't imagine how hard it would have been losing her at seven.

Shawn came back. "The coroner's ETA is now five minutes. I'm going to need a formal statement from you before you leave."

"Of course."

He looked at me for a moment. "I'm glad you were here."

I wasn't. I would have much preferred someone else finding the body, but I understood what he meant. "Shawn." I waited until I had his full attention. "I'm going to follow this wherever it goes. Even if it goes somewhere..." I looked over at Mayor Green, who was talking to one of her staff. "...uncomfortable."

He held my gaze steadily, and I could see him doing the same math I'd already done. Women were more likely to be killed by someone they knew or were intimate with, and spouses accounted for more than a third of those deaths. It was a very sturdy thread that led, directly or indirectly, back to the woman currently working her phone and caring very much about optics.

"I know," he said. "Just be careful. We don't want to make any accusations we can't take back."

I understood his position. Shawn's job was at the mercy of the mayor, but I couldn't worry about him. If the visions or evidence pointed at Green's family, then that was something he would have to live with. However, I would never accuse anyone of a crime unless I felt certain it could be proven. "Got it," I told him.

He looked up, his eyes widening. "Good. The coroner's here." He looked at Ezra. "Keep me updated." Then he left.

Ezra stood next to me, his arm brushing against mine.

"I can't believe I found another dead body," I said.

He looked at me sideways and quirked a brow.

"Don't," I told him.

He shrugged. "I didn't say anything."

"Your expression speaks volumes."

The corner of his mouth moved just barely, as if he were trying not to smile.

A scream from the crowd chilled me, and I heard Melissa Jones shout, "Gerry! Is that Gerry?" She was sobbing as she tried to get past the uniformed officers guarding the perimeter. "He did this to her," she accused, drawing everyone's attention to where she pointed. "Bash Green is low-life scum, and he killed my niece!"

Mayor Green's face turned the shade of a ripe beet as she watched the scene play out.

The way the crowd was staring between Bash and his mother, the mayor was going to be lucky if the incident didn't make statewide news.

So much for keeping things quiet.

CHAPTER SIX

There wasn't anything else I could do, so I gave my official statement, then walked back to Scents & Scentsability feeling completely discombobulated and tired. Part of it was surely the key lime carb load and finding Gerry dead, but I thought the anti-nausea shot was probably adding to my need for a nap.

The shop had three customers wandering around when I walked in. Pippa's smile faded when she looked at me. "Nora? Are you okay?"

I chuckled, but not like it was funny. "Not really," I told her honestly. "I don't think I'm going to be able to finish the day." I wasn't even sure I could drive myself home. My arms and legs felt like they were full of lead. I went to the back where I made my products and sat on the nearest stool, relieved to be off my feet.

A few minutes later, Pippa found me. "What's wrong? Did you judge the pie contest? Did something happen?"

"Yes, to all of the above." I scrubbed my face. I didn't sugarcoat my next words, because I knew Pippa didn't need it. "Someone was killed. I found her body."

"Of course you did," she said with more sympathy than sarcasm. "Only you could turn a gesture of goodwill into an investigation."

I was too tired to argue with her about something that was inherently true. "She was so young."

"Oh, Nora." Pippa leaned over and gave me a hug. "Why don't you go home?"

"A paramedic gave me a shot of Zofran, an antinausea medication, because I was throwing up pie. It's knocking me for a loop. I don't want to risk driving."

"I'm here!" Gilly shouted from the front of the shop.

"In the back," Pippa called out.

I glanced at Pippa.

She shrugged. "I texted her when you wandered back here looking all pitiful and pathetic."

"Nora, you look terrible," Gilly said when she saw me. "What happened?"

I told her about Gerry, the visions, the mayor, Bash, the pie tasting, and the throwing up of the pie tasting. Yuck.

Gilly looked on the verge of tears. "What will happen to her little girl?"

It wasn't a question any of us could answer. I assumed that as long as Bash wasn't arrested for murder, he would probably assume custody of their daughter.

Pippa patted my arm when I yawned with more force than felt good. "I can close for a little while and take you home."

"Nah." I was hoping the drug would wear off shortly so I wouldn't have to leave my car in town. "I'll just hang out back here, if that's all right."

"I have a better idea," Gilly said. "Come over to the spa and sleep on one of the massage beds for a little while. A few hours of sleep, binaural beats, and aromatherapy, and you'll be right as rain."

"Making everything right as rain seems like a big ask." I forced a smile. "But I'll gratefully take the bed."

THE SPA SMELLED LIKE EUCALYPTUS, sandalwood, and lavender, and I was thankful that none of the scents took me anywhere. It was a big reason I hadn't spent much time in Gilly's spa since it opened. I worried about picking up glimpses from her oncology patients more than anyone else. It had been years since my mother died, but for whatever reason, I'd been feeling more fragile than usual lately. I had an appointment with my gynecologist at the end of the month and planned to ask her about getting my hormones and bloodwork checked. Gilly had been sending me videos and articles on new studies coming out about the benefits of complete hormone replacement therapy. Since I was only on the estrogen patch, I figured it couldn't hurt to discuss it with my doctor.

That was a problem for another day. Right now, I needed to lie down and close my eyes.

Gilly had converted the front half of Lem's old antique shop into something that felt like a vacation spa escape. The walls were the color of warm sand, with accents in blush and pale sage, and the warm lighting was soothing like candlelight. Soft instrumental music drifted from a small speaker near the front desk, piped into all the rooms. Carly, one of Gilly's new therapists, was checking in a client with the serene efficiency of someone who had mastered the art of making other people feel calm. Potted succulents lined the windowsill. A small diffuser on the reception counter sent a thin curl of vapor into the air.

Gilly led me past the treatment rooms to the relaxation area in the back, a quiet room with two low massage beds dressed in crisp linens the color of green sea glass. She dimmed the lights to a soft amber glow, clicked on the binaural beats from a sound machine on the side table, and laid a thin blanket over me before I'd even fully settled.

"Do you want me to turn the bed warmer on?" she asked.

I had an internal heater that ran on high these days, so I shook my head. "I'm good." The massage table was padded but firm, a little firmer than I liked, but comfortable enough for a temporary respite.

I closed my eyes and felt Gilly's fingers brush hair away from my face. "Sleep," she said. "I'll check on you in a bit."

Relaxing, I drifted in the particular half-consciousness of a body that was too tired to stay awake but too wired to let go completely. The binaural beats were gentle and oddly soothing. I wasn't someone who put a lot of stock in holistic healing, but I thought maybe there was something to sounds rewiring your energy, even if only for a little while. The aromatherapy was ylang ylang, sweet bergamot, and vanilla, a combination scent called Relax Awhile. I knew this because I was the one who'd made it for Gilly.

I must have eventually drifted off, because I woke up to Gilly giving my shoulder a slight shake. "Hey, you," she said. "How are you feeling?"

"Clearer." I pushed myself up onto one elbow. "Still tired."

"The Zofran will do that." She passed me a small bottle of water from the side table. "Drink. When I had that diverticulitis flare-up in November, they gave it to me for nausea, and I was out for nine hours after Scott got me home."

"How long was I out?"

"Four hours, give or take."

"Gilly, it's past closing," I said. "You should've woken me up sooner."

"Awww." She pinched my cheek. "But you're so cute when you're sleeping."

"Hah." I rolled my eyes.

She handed me another bottle of water. "You're probably dehydrated. Drink it. You'll feel better."

"Yes, mother." I drank. She was right. It helped. I got up and slipped my shoes on, glad to be feeling steadier on my feet.

"So," she said. "Tell me about the contest. Before the part where it went sideways."

Going sideways was one way to describe murder. I almost laughed. "You want the pie part?"

"I want all of it."

I told her. The twenty-five pies, the scoring, number thirteen with its vanilla and the way it had surprised me, and number nineteen with the yuzu and the lattice crust that had been Gerry's. "Honestly, I think she had the best pie on the table," I said. "Lance scored her high too, from what he told me after. But Rob..." I shook my head. "Rob gave her a four, four, and a four. For the best pie there," I added incredulously. "I watched him do it."

Gilly's expression sharpened. "Rob Doyle is a dink."

"He was weird about the scoring as well. He wouldn't say which was his favorite after, as if he couldn't remember one pie from the other." I blinked as we walked out into the brighter hallway. "I don't know why he'd tank it. It's a pie contest. But eleven thousand dollars isn't nothing. The winner was a woman named Dora Charles, who I'd put solidly in the middle of the pack."

"Wait, what? Eleven thousand dollars? Girl! Are you kidding me?"

I shook my head. "Nope. That was the final prize pot."

"Well, dang. I better start working on my key lime pie recipe for next year."

"If there is a next year. This might be the first and last annual Key Lime Festival if it turns out the mayor was involved in any way."

"Bummer." Gilly methodically turned off lights as we made our way toward the reception area. "By the way, I've heard some extra juicy stuff about Rob Doyle."

"Really?" I looked at her. "What kind of things?"

"After you brought him up this morning, I had Amy Kinder, the zoning office secretary, in for a massage. I might have pushed the conversation forward by mentioning that my friend was judging the pie contest with Rob, and after a few minutes of my magic hands," she wiggled her fingers, "she started sharing the tea."

"Hot tea?" I asked.

Gilly grinned. "The hottest." She lifted a shoulder. "He's been on the town council long enough to have relationships with a lot of contractors and vendors. And from what she said, he's not above taking something on the side to make a decision on a city contract go a certain way."

"Bribes."

"That's a strong word for a strong rumor." She tilted her head. "But yes, that's the vibe she was dropping."

I thought about that. Rob Doyle, who had low-balled two standout pies, then disappeared from the grandstand before the publicity photos. Rob Doyle, whose name Melissa Jones had mentioned in the same breath as Lance Crabtree when she'd been worried about fairness. But even if he'd cheated on the scoring, he didn't have a motive to kill Gerry. Did he? "I can't figure out what he'd get out of making sure Gerry didn't win. It's not like Dora Charles is paying him off for a pie ribbon."

"Unless someone was paying him to make sure Gerry didn't win."

We looked at each other.

"Mayor Green," I said. I thought about the tight smile, the eyes that hadn't moved when Green had said Gerry's name into the microphone. "But then why not the third-place winner Sandy? Her pie was so much better than the winner's. I feel like Dora

Charles winning is the most random thing ever, or it was somehow planned."

"It sounds like we should maybe find out more about this Dora Charles."

I arched a brow at Gilly. "Are you the same woman who implored me not to find trouble when we took that cruise?"

"We were on vacation, Nora!"

"True." I giggled. "Okay, so we find out more about Dora Charles." I took my keys from my purse as we exited the building, Gilly locking up behind us. I was trying to think about who Gerry might have been afraid of. Someone she owed money to? Someone blackmailing her because of her ties to the mayor, or for some other reason? Or maybe she'd had a lover as well. "You said this morning that Bash had a reputation. That he'd always been a player." I paused. "Have you heard anything about Gerry? On that front?"

Gilly was quiet for a moment, which with Gilly meant she was choosing her words. "I've heard," she said carefully, "that Bash might not have been the only one."

I looked at her.

"Nothing specific," she said. "No name. Just that someone thought Gerry might have had something going on the side. Maybe started before the marriage ended, maybe after. But it seemed more like malicious gossip than anything based in truth."

I turned that over. . She'd been angry with Bash, right in his face on the courthouse lawn without flinching. Whatever she'd been afraid of had come from somewhere else, someone she'd spotted across the crowd after she'd already turned away from her soon-to-be ex-husband. "What if it wasn't about the divorce at all? What if she was having an affair and things went south?"

Gilly's eyes were steady on mine. "A married man, maybe. Someone with a lot to lose."

"Someone who'd want to make sure she stayed quiet." I thought about Melissa's words. After this weekend, you won't have to worry about him ever again. "I'm going to need to talk to Melissa again. She knows something about the mystery man."

"How are you feeling now?" Gilly asked when we got to our cars.

"Much better."

"Not sleepy?"

"No," I told her. "Wide awake."

"Plans for tonight?"

"Ezra is probably going to be working late." I eyed her suspiciously. "Why?"

"Scott is working the night shift at the hospital, so I thought maybe we could pick up some food and go see Melissa. Offer our condolences."

"And snoop around?"

Gilly's eyes widened and she pressed her fingers to her chest. "Why, Nora Black, I would never." Her eyes narrowed. "But you definitely would."

She had me there. "You would too."

"Let's go home first and clean up." She wrinkled her nose. "Maybe hit that mouth with a toothbrush."

I almost choked on a laugh. "I hate you sometimes."

She smirked. "No, you don't."

I shook my head. No, I didn't. I dug a piece of gum out of my purse and popped it into my mouth before starting up my car. It would have to do until I got home. I felt better with a plan, and I was glad Gilly was coming along. Melissa had been weird about the pie contest, and not just in a "I want to help my niece" kind of way. I needed her to fill in the blanks so I could get a sense of the whole puzzle. I hoped she was willing. If not, well, maybe my nose could pick up whatever she was avoiding putting down.

CHAPTER SEVEN

I made it home in under twenty minutes, showered, brushed my teeth twice, and changed into something that didn't smell like porta-potty and regret. By the time Gilly pulled up in her white SUV, I felt approximately sixty percent human, which was a significant improvement.

"You look better," she said when I climbed in.

"The bar was very low."

She'd changed into wide-leg jeans and a soft coral top, her chestnut hair down around her shoulders, and she looked, as always, like she'd spent approximately no effort achieving casual glamour. I'd worn jeans as well, with a loose cotton button-down in pale green that I hoped said we're just dropping by to be good neighbors, not interrogating you.

"Grocery store first," I said. "We can't show up empty-handed."

"Already ahead of you." She pointed to the back seat, where a white bakery box sat from Garden Cove's only grocery with a decent bakery counter. "Sock-It-to-Me bundt cake. I grabbed it on my way home."

I looked at her. "When did you have time?"

She lifted an eyebrow. "I'm a master multitasker."

"Yes, you are."

The Joneses lived in Millbrook Estates, the subdivision on the east side of Garden Cove where the houses had three-car garages and irrigation systems and the kind of landscaping that required a professional crew. The streets curved in gentle arcs past brick mailboxes and motion-sensor lights, and every lawn looked like it had been checkered. The things landscapers could do these days were amazing, and amazing didn't come cheap.

Gilly pulled into the driveway of a large colonial with a wide front porch and two potted topiaries flanking the columns on either side of the front door. Warm light glowed from the windows.

Edgar answered the door before we'd finished knocking. He was in a cardigan and dress slacks, holding a glass of water, and his face did the thing it always did when he saw me — it lit up. "Nora," he said. Then he saw Gilly and his smile widened. "And you've brought a friend. Come in, come in."

"We don't want to intrude," I said. "We just wanted to bring something over and offer our condolences."

Edgar took the bakery box from Gilly with both hands, and I saw him read the label. Eagerness tinged with anxiety colored his expression. "That's very thoughtful," he said. "Melissa is in the family room. She's..." He paused. "She's not really up for a lot of company tonight. But come in. I know she'll want to see you."

He led us through the entry, past the living room impeccably decorated for a magazine shoot, and into a back area that was cozier and more comfortable. It had cream walls, dark wood accents, and built-in shelving lined with books organized by color. On a large, oversized chaise in the corner, Melissa was curled under a cream knit throw blanket, a book in hand, her hair loose and her eyes red-rimmed. On either side of her, nestled into the folds of the blanket, were two small Shih

Tzus, one silvery-white and one tan, both apparently asleep.

They were asleep until Gilly said, "Oh, Melissa, I'm so sorry," and then both dogs launched off the chaise in a frenzy of barking and scrambling paws, skittering across the hardwood toward us.

I took a step back. Not because they were threatening — they were the size of throw pillows — but because they were fast and it startled me.

"Daisy is deaf and Button is blind," Melissa said, with the slightly automated quality of someone who has said this to every visitor for years. "They'll calm down in a minute."

"No worries at all," I said, crouching to let the tan one sniff my hand. It sneezed on me, then began wagging with its entire body.

True to Melissa's word, they settled within moments, circling back to the chaise and reclaiming their spots.

I sat on the couch closest to Melissa's chaise. Gilly caught my eye and tilted her head almost imperceptibly toward the door.

"Edgar," she said, turning to him with a warm smile, "why don't you show me where to put the cake? I'd love to see your kitchen."

Edgar, who was not a complicated man, nodded

and led her out of the room, and just like that, Melissa and I were alone.

She had a box of tissues on the end table and a small pile of used ones in her lap. She didn't seem embarrassed by it. Grief had a way of humbling pride.

"Have they arrested Bash yet?" she asked.

"I don't know," I told her. "But I don't think so."

"He did it." She said it as if it were a fact.

"What makes you so certain?"

"He was furious when she asked for the divorce."

"I thought he was the one who cheated."

"He was." There was a flash of something fierce in Melissa's red-rimmed eyes. "He got caught, so Gerry kicked him out. She wasn't going to stay with someone who treated her like that." The pride in her voice was unmistakable. "She had more self-respect than that."

"Is he still with the secretary?"

Melissa threw up a hand. "Oh, who knows. Does it matter?"

I let a moment pass. One of the dogs, Daisy or Button, I'd already lost track, climbed up next to me on the couch and put its chin on my thigh with the confidence of a cutie who'd never been told no. I scratched behind its ear.

"Was Gerry seeing anyone?" I asked casually.

Melissa's eyes sharpened. "What are you asking?"

"Only that she was young and pretty," I said. "I'm sure there were people interested in her."

"Evie was her main priority." The words came out clipped and final, not quite an answer. "That little girl was the only company she needed."

After that, something in Melissa closed off. She was still polite, still grateful we'd come, but her answers got shorter and her gaze trailed off whenever I spoke. I gave her my condolences again, told her to call if she needed anything, and went to find Gilly.

The kitchen was at the back of the house. Edgar was at the island, and Gilly was leaning against the counter across from him with the easy conversational posture of a woman who could make anyone feel like she'd known them for years. Edgar had cut himself a slice of the bundt cake and was eating it with visible, guilty pleasure.

And then I noticed it. This was the kitchen from my vision. The one I'd had last night at Tres Mujeres. The countertops, the cabinet color, the layout — all of it matched what I'd seen in the vision triggered by the scent of yuzu on Melissa's sleeve.

Edgar held a bite of cake up on his fork and said to me, "Don't tell my doctor." He ate the portion, and when he finished chewing, he added, "She wants me to cut back on simple carbohydrates. No sugar."

"I saw nothing," I said.

He pointed his fork at me. "You're a good woman, Nora Black."

"Thanks," I told him, though I wasn't sure that keeping his cake secret made me good or bad. "Was Gerry staying here with you and Melissa?" I asked, once again trying for casual and hoping it would land.

He nodded, chewing. "Only for a couple of weeks. Having Evie here has been wonderful, actually. That little girl is a pistol."

"Where is Evie now?" Gilly asked.

Edgar's expression shifted, just slightly. "Bash kept her after the festival broke up." He set his fork down. "I don't like it, but there's not much we can do tonight."

A clear glass bottle on the counter caught my eye. Yuzu juice, the same brand I'd seen in the vision at the restaurant. I drifted toward it, picked it up, and unscrewed the cap under the pretense of reading the label.

I inhaled, focusing my aroma mojo on the sharp floral citrus that hit me immediately.

The kitchen is bright. Two people at the island, their faces blurred. The woman has an apron on and is measuring yuzu juice into a bowl. By voice, it's Melissa.

"Come on, sweetheart," Edgar says. He sounds tired. "You can't always bail her out of trouble. The girl won't learn if we don't let her figure some things out for herself."

She stirs the yuzu into the mixture. "I promised Gloria I would always take care of her."

"Sweetheart." Edgar wraps his arms around her from behind. "Ten thousand dollars is a significant debt to take care of."

"That's why I'm helping her win. This pie recipe won the Florida Key Lime Grand Prix." Her voice is certain. "There's not another pie in town that will come close. She'll get the top prize and then she won't have to worry anymore."

"Until the next time." He releases her. "You have to stop."

"Don't worry. I have a plan." She keeps her eyes on the bowl. "I'll teach her how to make this pie, and it won't use up our resources."

"Melissa." His voice drops. "I can't get another call

from the regional branch supervisor about the overdrafts."

She kisses his cheek. "You won't. I promise."

"What did you do?" he asks.

Melissa doesn't answer. She just keeps stirring.

I wobbled coming out of the vision and braced myself with a hand on the counter. I set the bottle down and carefully put the cap back on. Edgar and Gilly were both looking at me.

"Does this need to be refrigerated after opening?" I asked, tapping the bottle.

Edgar blinked. "I honestly have no idea. That's Melissa's territory." He studied me for a moment. "Is something wrong?"

"No, no," I assured him. "It's all good." I gestured to Gilly. "We better get going." I snapped my fingers before we could leave. "Oh, hey. Do you know a woman named Dora Charles?"

Edgar knew a lot of people. Being a bank manager in a town like Garden Cove was essentially a social obligation. He didn't even hesitate. "Dora. Yes. She's a sales supervisor over at Hastings Tires. Nice enough woman."

And an average baker, I thought. I'd driven past Hastings plenty of times, but I always went to the

Jiffy Lube closer to downtown for my car needs. "Thanks," I said.

He had no follow-up questions about why I was asking, and I didn't know if I found that suspicious or if he was just the kind of man who lacked curiosity. I decided it was probably the latter.

We said our goodbyes a few minutes later. Melissa had moved to the kitchen by then, wrapped in her blanket with both dogs trailing behind her, and she hugged me at the door with more feeling than I'd expected, her grip tight for a moment before she let go.

In the car, Gilly waited until we'd cleared the subdivision before she said, "Well?"

"Ten thousand dollars," I said. "Gerry had a ten-thousand-dollar debt. Melissa was going to help her win the contest to clear it."

Gilly's hands tightened on the wheel. "That's why she wanted to be a judge."

"And why she was so furious when Leila pulled her." I looked out the window at the passing streetlights. "She wasn't just being a protective aunt. She had a plan, and Leila dismantled it."

"What kind of debt?"

"I don't know. The memory didn't give me that." I paused. "But Edgar mentioned overdrafts. Whatever Melissa's been doing to help Gerry financially, it's been coming out of their accounts."

Gilly chewed on the inside of her cheek for a moment, then said, "And then the prize went to Dora Charles."

"Who sells tires for a living and apparently bakes a very average pie."

Gilly was quiet for a moment. "If Melissa was planning to help Gerry win, and the contest was rigged to make sure she didn't, and now Gerry is dead..." She let the sentence trail off in the way she did when she didn't want to say the obvious thing.

"I know," I said.

Tomorrow was Sunday. Hastings Tires was almost certainly closed. I pulled out my phone and called Ezra. It rang four times before he picked up, sounding like a man who had been having a very long day and expected it to get longer.

"Hey," I said. "I need you to look someone up for me. Dora Charles. She works at Hastings Tires." I paused. "And I need to tell you about a vision I had."

"Of course you do," he said warmly. "If it's not urgent, you can tell me about it tonight. I'll come over."

"Perfect," I told him.

"Give me an hour."

"I'll make coffee."

"And pie?" he teased.

I groaned. "No pie ever again."

He chuckled. "Love you."

"Love you back." I put the phone away and looked out at the dark road ahead. Somewhere in Garden Cove, a seven-year-old named Evie was with her father, and nobody knew yet whether that was safe or not. Melissa was keeping secrets that could hold the key to finding her niece's killer, and there was the matter of the ten-thousand-dollar debt.

And why had Dora Charles won eleven thousand dollars with a perfectly unremarkable pie?

None of it made sense yet. Maybe after talking to Ezra tonight, we'd be able to fit a few pieces together.

CHAPTER
EIGHT

Ezra arrived at nine-thirteen. I heard his car in the driveway and had the front door open before he reached the porch steps. It had been a long day, and I was in serious need of a hug.

The sleeves of his dress shirt were rolled to the elbows, and his hair had been run through by his hands enough times that the curl at his ears was more pronounced than usual. He looked at me in the doorway and I could see some of the tension ease from his expression.

"Hey," he said.

"Hey, yourself." I stepped into his arms, not waiting for him to get inside. He folded me in, and I inhaled him like a lifeline. Gosh, he always smelled so good. After a few unrushed moments, I let him go and pulled him inside.

"Coffee's made," I told him. "No pie, but I have a jar of Gilly's jam if you want toast or a PB and J."

Ezra shook his head. "I ate at the station." I held his hand as we walked into the kitchen. "How are you feeling? Pippa texted that you were zonked when you got back to the shop."

"I'm pretty sure it was the shot Bob gave me. It helped with the nausea, but it knocked me out." I poured two mugs of coffee. "No worries, though. It wore off hours ago. I had a nice nap at Gilly's spa and woke up fine." I slid one of the coffees across the island to him.

"Good." He dumped a healthy dose of sugar into his mug, then took a sip. "Tell me about your day first. The parts I wasn't there for."

So I told him, starting from the beginning. Gilly's kitchen in the morning, the strawberry jam, the conversation about Gerry and Bash and the affair rumor that wasn't quite a rumor. I told him about the contest and the twenty-five pies, Rob's scoring patterns, Lance's comment about giving Gerry's pie high marks, the way the results had landed wrong for everyone standing in front of that grandstand. I told him about the Joneses' house,

Melissa on the chaise with her dogs, Edgar and his bundt cake, and the kitchen that turned out to be the kitchen from my vision.

"When I went into the kitchen, there was a bottle of yuzu juice on the counter. The same scent that triggered the first vision, the one I told you about at the restaurant. I opened it and got another memory." I set my own mug down and took him through it carefully. "Edgar said, or implied, that Gerry had been in debt, and that Melissa had been bailing her out for a while. He basically put his foot down about Melissa lending Gerry ten thousand dollars. He said she needed to learn how to solve her own problems. Melissa, on the other hand, was sure she had it all covered."

He'd listened without interrupting, which was one of the many things about Ezra that I really loved. "I know you have questions," I said. "Give them to me."

Ezra gave me a serious look. "Ten thousand dollars is a significant debt."

I nodded. "And Melissa's plan to cover it wasn't financial. She said it wouldn't use their resources. Whatever she was going to do, it was leverage. Not money." I paused. "Edgar asked her what she'd done and she didn't answer. She just kept stirring."

"She blackmailed someone."

"That's what I think. And it had to be one of the judges. That's the only thing that makes sense, right? She couldn't influence the scoring directly once Leila pulled her from the panel. So she found someone on the panel she had some influence with or over." I watched him. "Rob was working against Gerry somehow." I gave Ezra a look. "Did you find him? Was he sick too?"

Ezra gave a quick nod. "We found him. He wasn't sick. He was watching the pie eating contest with half the town."

"Ick. I would've barfed all over again." I shook my head. "Anyway, I think Rob rigged it for Dora Charles to win. So not Rob. Certainly not me. Which leaves Lance."

Ezra put his mug down with a deliberateness that was its own kind of tell.

"Lance told me he'd given Gerry's pie high marks. I never saw his actual sheet, but the math of her second-place finish supports it. Without tens she doesn't place that well given Rob's scoring. He did his part."

"Lance's wife was with him right after the judging, and he was throwing up in a stall several toilets away when Gerry was killed," Ezra said. "The other two men, Brandon Carroll and Frank Wright, both backed him up on that. He gave a brief statement, then left with her. They both looked pretty shaken up."

"Maybe the place she thought she'd rigged was in the people who were counting the scores."

"You think she got pencil whipped?"

"Maybe." The kitchen was quiet for a moment as we both considered alternatives.

Finally, Ezra reached across the island and put his hand over mine. After a moment, I turned my hand over and held his. "My turn to listen," I told him.

He smiled, then nodded. "From my end of things, there is some new information. First, I got Dora Charles's address and called her to set up a time for us to interview her tomorrow at ten."

I gave him a thankful look. I hated getting up early on Sundays.

He continued. "Also, the coroner noted a contusion on her skull at the scene. The injury is consistent with a hard flat surface. From the abrasions, it looks like brick, possibly, or poured concrete. Not the interior walls of a portable toilet." He paused. "We're canvassing the courthouse and its surroundings tomorrow to see if we can find any evidence of where the blow to her head might have happened. It could have been an accident, of course, but the coroner says the impact was significant. He won't know the full extent of the damage until the proper medical examination, and that won't happen until tomorrow."

"The head injury wasn't what killed her, right?"

"Not directly," Ezra said. "There was too much evidence that she'd been suffocated. After her body was moved to the morgue and lividity set in, bruises showed up around her mouth, nose, and cheeks. But the coroner said the head injury probably made her disoriented and easier to subdue."

I thought about the moment she'd raised her hand from the bakers' group when her name was called for second place. She'd looked pale and sick. I'd assumed it was about losing. Now it sounded like she'd been operating with a concussion.

"We got one lucky break, though it doesn't give us a lot more information." He reached into his jacket pocket and pulled out his phone, turning it to face me. "She had her phone on her, and our IT guys managed to get it unlocked. I photographed the texts."

I looked at the photo he pulled up. A text

message, outgoing, to a number labeled only with a string of digits. No contact name.

I know you're here. Last stall. Now. We need to talk.

I read it twice. "Was it timestamped?" I asked.

"Eighteen minutes before you found her."

"That would have been right after the winners were announced."

"It's a short window of opportunity." He nodded. "But it's pretty clear that she invited her killer to meet her."

"That's awful."

He put the phone on the counter between us. "Yeah, but it confirms this was someone she knew, and knew well enough to be texting on a burner phone."

I thought about the moment on the lawn before the pie contest. Gerry going white. Reversing direction. Pushing past Bash like he wasn't even a factor.

"She saw someone," I said. "On the lawn, before all this. She looked scared."

"Tell me exactly what you saw."

"She was arguing with Bash near the grandstand. She turned to walk away, then she stopped. Something across the lawn caught her eye and she went pale." I met his gaze. "Genuinely pale — the color left her face — and then she turned, pushing past Bash, in the opposite direction. Not running but definitely moving with purpose."

"Which direction?"

I thought about it. "Toward the crowd."

Ezra nodded slowly. "Do you think that's the person she texted?"

"Maybe," I said. "But she looked like whoever it was, it was the last person she wanted to see, so I'm not sure."

I looked at the text again. *We need to talk.* Not a question. Not a request. A demand.

"There's more on the phone," Ezra said. "We haven't done a full extraction yet. The techs will be working on it over the next couple of days. But the screen showed a history of incoming texts from the same unregistered number going back six months. No name was ever used. Only a nickname." He paused. "Snoopy."

I blinked. "Snoopy?"

"A lot of contact on his end. Very little response on hers in the last two months." He huffed out a breath. "What kind of nickname is Snoopy?"

"I don't know, Easy," I teased, calling him by the nickname his friends used. "You tell me."

He rewarded me with an adorable crooked smile.

"That's the first two letters of my name, so it makes perfect sense."

I laughed. "If you say so. Hey, maybe Snoopy is a play on our mystery man's name. Snoopy. Snooooopy. S. N." I quit before I said something I couldn't take back. "I've got nothing."

He leaned over and gave my tush a squeeze. "You've got a cute butt."

"I'm not sure that's going to help the case."

He grinned. "It'll help my case."

"Oh? What case is that?"

"My bad case of loving you."

I don't know how I managed it, but I groaned and laughed at the same time. "So cheesy."

He gave me a kiss, his lips tasting of sweet black coffee and him. "The cheesiest," he agreed. "But still true."

His eyes softly examining my face made my pulse quicken. Ezra picked up both our mugs and put them in the sink.

I came around the island and leaned into him. He held me, resting his chin on the top of my head.

"I hate this one," I said into his chest.

"I know." He rubbed my back. "We're going to figure it out."

I believed him. Not because he was trying to

reassure me but because he was Ezra, and he wouldn't stop until we did.

"How about I take you to bed, and we can both forget about all this for a little while?"

I tilted my head up. "That's the best suggestion I've heard all day."

He kissed me, sweet at first, then less sweet, in a way that verged on filthy.

I loved it. "Okay, stud. Take me to bed."

Sunday morning was going to come with a fresh set of problems. But tonight, at least, for a little while, I was going to let them go.

CHAPTER NINE

Dora Charles lived in a yellow craftsman bungalow on Persimmon Street, four blocks from the square, with a front porch that had two rocking chairs and a wind chime made of large bamboo reeds. There were flower boxes under the windows with early spring pansies in purple and white, and a welcome mat that said *Come Back With A Warrant*, which, given the morning's agenda, I found faintly amusing.

Ezra didn't comment on the mat. He rang the bell.

Dora Charles answered the door in jeans and a flannel shirt with her red hair pulled back, and she looked like a woman who had not slept particularly well. She was tall, and she had an open, readable face that makes a person either very trustworthy or very bad at keeping secrets. Possibly both.

"Detective Holden," she said. Then when she saw me, her eyes widened with recognition. "And Nora Black." She gestured in my direction. "You were on the judging panel yesterday."

"I was," I said. "You made a beautiful pie, Dora."

Her brow furrowed at the compliment. "Thank you. Come in."

The house smelled like key lime.

I registered this without letting it show. She'd been baking. Stress baking, judging from the mess in the kitchen as we passed on the way to the living room. A pie was cooling on a rack near the window, the custard the pale yellow-green of a good key lime, the meringue simple and unembellished. Not a contest pie. Just a pie.

We sat in the living room. Dora offered coffee and pie. Ezra accepted and I declined, because the memory of twenty-five key lime bites fighting their way out of my body was too fresh.

"So, Ms. Charles," Ezra said, starting the conversation. "First let me congratulate you on winning the pie contest yesterday."

Her cheeks and neck developed pink splotches.

"Thanks," she replied without meeting his gaze. "I got lucky, I guess."

"Hmm," he said. "Lucky." He kept his eyes trained on her. "What made you decide to enter?"

"I've always loved baking." The way she said it, I believed her. "So, I thought, why not? I thought it would be fun."

"Fun." Ezra made a show of jotting the word down on the notes app in his phone. "Did you see the deceased, Geraldine Green, at any time before or after the judging?"

"No," she blurted. "I only saw her when the top three winners were announced."

I cleared my throat. I wanted to get a better look at her kitchen and see if I could sniff anything out. "Do you mind if I get some water?" I touched my throat. "I'm a little dry this morning."

She flapped her hand in the air. "Go ahead. The glasses are over the sink."

I got up and walked back toward the front where we'd passed on the way in. As I got to the sink, the fragrant lime notes hit me immediately, bright and sharp. I inhaled slowly, the way I'd learned to inhale when I needed to jumpstart my visions. I opened myself to whatever came. The strongest memory surged to the foreground. I braced against the counter and welcomed it in.

The kitchen is bright with afternoon light. Yellow curtains, the rooster on the wall. A tall redhead is at the counter rolling out pastry dough, her hands working the surface with the easy rhythm of long practice. A bowl of fresh-squeezed key lime juice sits at her elbow.

There's a knock at the door.

She wipes her hands on a dish towel and goes to answer it.

Rob Doyle's voice reaches the kitchen before his blurry face and body appear.

"Dora. Hope I'm not interrupting."

"Rob." She steps back. "No, come in. I'm just working on my entry for the contest."

He comes into the kitchen and looks at the counter, the bowl, the half-rolled dough. He picks up a key lime from the bowl and turns it in his hand.

"That's actually what I wanted to talk to you about. The final ticket count came in this afternoon," he says. "The prize pool is going to be significant. Very significant."

She's wiping flour from her hands, slowly. "How significant?"

"Thousands of dollars," he says. "And I'm one of the judges. You're a good baker, Dora." He sets the key lime

back in the bowl. "Be a shame if a really excellent pie didn't get the recognition it deserved."

Silence.

"I'm not going to cheat," she says.

"It wouldn't be the first time."

"And the split?"

"Fifty-fifty sounds fair. I'll be taking all the risk."

"It's a good pie, Rob."

"I know it is," he says. "That's why I'm here."

I stepped back from the counter, getting my bearings.

Dora was in the kitchen doorway. "You find everything all right?"

"I did," I assured her. "I took a glass down and filled it with tap water." I held it up toward her then took a drink. "Thanks."

I followed her back into the living room and sat down next to Ezra. He gave me an assessing look.

I nodded, then gave him a little wink.

"So," I said genially. "How well do you know Rob Doyle?"

Her brow dipped and her eyes narrowed. "Well enough." She straightened some magazines on her coffee table. "We've crossed paths. Town business, you know how it is."

"Hastings Tires does city vehicle work, doesn't it?" Ezra said.

She looked at him, then glanced away. "That's right."

"And Doyle's been helpful with those contracts?" I asked.

Dora chewed her upper lip for a moment but didn't answer.

I decided to push the narrative. "Rob already told us that he fixed the judging so that you'd win."

Her brows went up. "I don't believe you."

"He said he came over a couple days ago and offered you a fifty-fifty split, if you would go along with it. He said you two have done some shady deals in the past, so he knew you'd be up for it."

Dora looked as green as I'd felt the day before. Her expression was one of bewilderment and fear. "He...I can't believe..."

Ezra's eyes were on me now. I raised a brow and gave a slight shrug.

"You might as well tell us, Ms. Charles. Otherwise, it's his word against yours," he told her in an official tone.

"Fine, fine." She had tears in her eyes now. Her shoulders slumped and her voice was resigned. "He came over two days ago, and he asked me if he made sure my pie won, would I split the pot with him." She leaned back and put the back of her shaking hand over her eyes. "We've had understandings before. For the city contracts." She let out a soft moan then sat up straight. "Will I be charged with something?"

"Fraud, possibly," Ezra said. "It will be up to the DA."

"The money. I was planning on giving it back." Her eyes were red and glassy. "I felt so awful after that woman died. I haven't been able to sleep at all since then." She scrubbed her face. "I'm so tired. I didn't even want to do it."

At the door, she looked at me. "Did you really think my pie was good?"

I thought about pie number nineteen. The lattice crust, the yuzu, the flawless buttery pastry. I thought about the tens I'd given it without hesitation.

"Yours was a good pie," I said honestly, because none of them had been terrible.

Ezra told her to keep the conversation private, and not to leave town, then we said goodbye and walked to the car.

Ezra waited until we'd cleared Persimmon Street before he said anything.

"So, Rob approaches her the day before the contest?" he asked.

"When the prize money was already in the thousands," I said. "He saw the number and decided a little cheating was worth the risk."

"And she agreed because they'd done business before."

"Yep." I looked out the window, looking at houses as we made our way downtown. "Rob knew she wouldn't say no. He knew she couldn't afford to."

Ezra turned left toward the station. "The pie scheme and the contract bribe. Neither of them can report the other without ratting out their own involvement."

"Except she just did."

"Except she just did." He glanced at me. "Thanks to my clever partner."

"More like my clever nose." I shook my head. "Sakes alive. Leila is not going to be happy. She was so proud of this festival. Now it's rife with a cheating scandal and murder."

Ezra's phone rang through the car speakers. He answered on the first ring.

"Hey, boss," Broyles said, his voice filling the car. "You're going to want to come to the corner of Courthouse Square and Maple. The barbershop. Clive's Clippers."

"What have you got?"

"Security footage from across the street. From yesterday afternoon. During the contest." He stopped for a moment. "You're going to want to see it in person. Trust me on that."

Ezra's eyes cut to mine for a half second. "We're eight minutes out."

CLIVE'S CLIPPERS WAS a barbershop that had been on the corner of Courthouse Square and Maple for thirty-one years according to the sign in the window. Broyles held the door open for us. The owner, a compact man in his sixties named Clive Okafor, stood near the back counter.

Reese, standing next to him, gave me a brief nod. She looked...pissed off. What had they caught on the camera?

Broyles took us to the back office, a small room wedged between the storage shelves and a mini fridge with an insurance magnet stuck to it. Reese didn't follow.

I braced myself. This was going to be bad.

The security system monitor sat on a cluttered desk, the footage already queued. The timestamp in the corner put it at twelve forty-seven in the afternoon. Saturday. That was about the time I was somewhere around pie number eight or nine, wondering what the heck I was doing with my life.

"Clive's camera covers the side and rear of the courthouse," Broyles said. "Angle's not perfect but it's enough."

He hit play.

Gerry came into frame first. She was moving the way she'd been moving when I watched her on the lawn, quick and determined. Bash was right behind her, catching up, and even with the slightly grainy film, I could tell he was angry.

They argued. Gerry was gesturing, controlled and precise. Bash cut the air with his arms, his gestures growing larger and more unpredictable.

Then Bash's right hand moved like a snake striking its prey.

He grabbed the top of her head, then drove it back into the brick wall of the courthouse.

I gasped as my throat knotted and my mouth

went dry, helpless to do anything but watch as Gerry slid down the wall, her legs buckling under her.

I blinked back tears. Bash hadn't even flinched. If this had been an accident or the first time he'd hurt Gerry, he would have tried to help her up. He didn't. Instead, he loomed over her, his hand balled in a fist.

My stomach clenched with dread.

Gerry sat against the brick looking dazed. Bash stood over her. He drew his right fist back, cocked at his hip. Gerry's arms came up in defense, her face turned away. The reflexive action of someone who had seen that fist before. Probably many times over many years.

Bash didn't throw the punch. He held the fist for a long moment, looking down at her. Then he lowered it. His mouth moved and he said something, a sentence or two. After, he turned and walked out of frame.

Gerry stayed against the wall for a few seconds longer. Then she put one hand flat on the brick behind her and used it to push herself upright. It took effort. She steadied herself against the wall with both hands, touched the back of her head once with her fingertips, looked at her fingers, and then straightened her shirt and staggered out of frame.

Broyles stopped the footage. There was a box of tissue on the desk, so I took a couple, wiped my eyes, and blew my nose. Seeing that footage made me even more sorry for Geraldine Green, and the life she'd been forced to endure.

Ezra stood with his arms at his sides and his jaw set. He looked at the frozen image on the monitor for a moment longer. He walked out of the office and pointed at Reese.

"McKay." His voice was even. Completely even. "Get Judge Horner on the line. We need an arrest warrant for Sebastian 'Bash' Green. Tell him it's for aggravated assault resulting in grievous bodily harm."

Reese had her phone out before he finished the sentence.

Broyles was already bagging the footage drive.

I stood at the desk with my hand still flat on the surface and thought about Gerry pushing herself up off a brick wall with her fingertips. Straightening her shirt before walking back to the grandstand. She had to have been in terrible shape, but she'd raised her hand when her name was called for second place. With a concussion, eleven thousand dollars slipping away from her. She must've been devastated.

Ezra rested his hand on my shoulder for a moment. Brief and steady.

"He won't get away with this," he told me.

"I hope not." I patted his hand. "I hope he gets what he deserves."

CHAPTER TEN

Bash Green had been arrested and was on his way to the station by mid-afternoon. The medical examiner had sent over his preliminary findings at Ezra's request.

"My gosh," Reese hissed, then she read it aloud. "Victim has multiple healed fractures, including the right ulna, remodeling of fractures in both hands. Two healed skull fractures. The ME notes that the injuries are consistent with repeated blunt force trauma over an extended period." She scratched her head. "What this woman went through. What a nightmare. Makes me sick."

"So awful," I agreed.

Reese muttered a curse and said, "I had to go down to our paper files, but I found a domestic disturbance report from eight years ago. Gerry had been pregnant at the time. The officer who responded noted injuries consistent with physical assault, including a bruised cheek and a bloody nose. Gerry had initially given a statement. Then she'd changed it the next day and said she fell. She refused to follow through with charges and the case went nowhere."

Eight years ago, pregnant, she'd reached for help once. And then Bash had gotten to her, told her whatever he'd told her, and she'd taken it back. And then eight more years of healed fractures.

"She was in a vulnerable spot," I said. There was more than one man who learned quickly that laying hands on me would land them in the hospital, or worse. I tried not to judge other people as if I was holding up a mirror, though. Not everyone was built the same, and that's what made the world go round.

The front doors opened and Bash Green, spitting mad and full of indignation, came in wearing handcuffs and flanked by two uniformed officers.

"This is harassment," he shouted. "My mother is the mayor of this town, and I will make sure each and every one of you loses your job."

"You'll be able to call your lawyer as soon as you've been processed," one of the officers said flatly. "Until then, you have the right to remain silent, so please, shut all the way up."

"Then I want to wait in a room. Not out here." He looked around the station. His gaze locked with mine for a moment. "Who are you?"

I wanted to tell him I was his worst nightmare, but I went with not saying anything at all. I avoided feeding trolls when possible.

He didn't like me ignoring him and called me an uncharitable name usually reserved for female dogs. I didn't even bother to look back up at him.

A small voice behind me said, "Is my dad coming back?"

I turned around.

Evie Green, seven years old, had her mother's brown hair and a pair of shoes with light-up soles that blinked when she shifted her weight. I hadn't seen the officers bring her in. She was sitting in one of the plastic chairs along the wall with a backpack on her lap and both hands wrapped around the straps. She watched her father disappear through the door with an expression that was mostly blank.

A young officer I didn't know well, Keisha Simmons, a first-year rookie, was crouched next to her. She glanced at me as if to ask, why does this feel so crappy?

“CPS has been called,” she said quietly. “It’s a Sunday, and they are short-handed, so they said it would be a couple hours. The little girl doesn’t know.”

“Doesn’t know...?”

“About her mom,” Keisha said. “They didn’t tell her.”

“Did you?”

“She shook her head. CPS said one their social worker would handle it.”

“Cripes.” I pulled out my phone and called Edgar, because I didn’t have Melissa’s number.

He answered on the second ring.

“Edgar, it’s Nora. Evie is at the station. She’s fine, she’s not hurt, but she’s waiting for CPS and she needs family here. Bash has been arrested. Can you and Melissa come sit with her?”

There was a sharp intake of breath, then Edgar said, “We’ll be there shortly.”

I sat down next to Evie.

She looked at me sideways. “You were at the pie contest.”

“I was,” I said. “I was one of the judges. Were you there?”

She nodded. “Until my pop-pop took me for ice cream.”

I wondered if she was talking about Edgar. "Your pop-pop sounds like a good man."

Evie nodded, satisfied, and looked back down at her backpack.

We sat for a moment. Keisha had straightened up and took a few steps back, giving us space.

The little girl shifted her weight and her shoes blinked. She was looking at things around the station—the water cooler, a plastic plant in the corner, the exit sign above the door—and I could see her mouth moving slightly.

"What are you playing?" I asked.

"Wig," she said, and pointed at a chair.

I looked at the chair. "What?"

She pointed again. "Chair. Hair. Hair is used to make wigs. So it's a wig."

"Oh," I said. "Okay. Let me try." I looked around. "Light. Bright. Evie, because Evie is bright."

Evie giggled. Her feet kicked. She shook her head. "That's a terrible one."

"I need to practice, huh?"

She nodded, solemn.

"Your mom teach you this game?"

"Mmhm." She pulled one of the backpack straps through her fingers. "When daddy yells or gets mad, it helps me to remember..." She scrunched her nose.

"She says it's how you remember the important things and let go of things that don't matter. You find the bridge."

"The bridge," I said.

"Chair to hair to wig. That's three bridges." She held up three fingers. "Two is better. One is best."

Across the room, Lance Crabtree came through the door and stopped when he saw me. His face had the annoyed look of a man who had been called in on his Sunday off. He caught my eye and gestured toward the hallway.

I looked at Evie. "Will you be okay for a minute?"

She nodded and went back to her bridges.

I crossed to Lance.

"Hey," he said, keeping his voice low. "Ezra filled me in on Doyle. Crazy, right?"

"Very," I said. "Is there anything legal that can be done about it?"

"He basically stole thousands of dollars." He glanced toward the back of the station. "And with the prior bribery added to the charges, he might see some serious time."

"Good," I said. If Rob hadn't robbed Gerry of her win, she might still be alive. I didn't say that out loud. But I thought it.

Lance nodded, and he was about to say something else when the front doors opened hard enough to announce themselves.

Allison Green came in like a tornado, ready to wipe us all out.

She was in a blazer, pressed slacks, heels on a Sunday, and she went straight past the front desk without stopping.

"I want my son released. Now!" she said to the room in general and no one in particular. Then she saw me. Her eyes stopped.

"Ms. Black." Her voice dropped a register. "I should've known you were behind this."

"Not this time." I shook my head. "Your son smashed his wife's head into a brick wall hard enough that she had a skull fracture. And because of that injury, she was too dazed to fight back when someone suffocated her a little while later."

"My son would never—"

"There's a recording of him doing exactly that." The footage played in my head uninvited and my stomach turned over. "The barbershop across from the courthouse has a security camera. His actions are on tape."

That took some of the wind out of her. She straightened her blazer.

"I want to see it," she said.

Lance stepped forward. "I can't allow that. You're the mother of the perpetrator in this case, not the mayor."

She turned on him. "I am always the mayor. Don't ever forget it."

She pulled her phone from her purse and walked away from us. I heard her say, "Chief Rafferty, I need you at the station. Now."

I looked at Lance.

He was pale under his tan, his jaw tight. He said he needed some air and walked toward the exit without waiting for a response.

I watched him go. The DA's office operated under the mayor's purview, the same as the chief of police. Lance had just told the mayor of Garden Cove no, in front of witnesses, on a case where her son was the subject of an arrest warrant.

I didn't envy him. I didn't trust him either, not entirely, not yet. But I didn't envy him.

"Gammy!"

I turned.

Melissa was coming through the front door, and Evie had launched herself out of the chair and thrown herself at her great-aunt. Melissa caught her and held on, her eyes closing for a moment over the top of Evie's head. It was telling that Evie felt safe and happy with Melissa, excited to see her, when she'd had barely any reaction when Allison Green, her actual grandmother, had barreled into the station.

Melissa looked at me over Evie's shoulder. Her eyes were red, but her jaw was set. She mouthed *thank you*.

I nodded.

Evie had her face buried in Melissa's neck, her shoes blinking steadily against the back of Melissa's coat. The station was loud with Bash's lawyer arriving at the front desk and Allison Green on her phone in the corner.

I stood in the middle of all of it and thought about bridges.

Find the bridge, and you find your way.

CHAPTER ELEVEN

I'd wanted to speak with Melissa alone, so Keisha took Evie into a nearby office to give us privacy. We sat in some chairs near the hallway, close enough to the room where Evie was waiting but far enough from the noise of the front desk. Melissa sat with her back straight and her hands folded in her lap.

"She doesn't know yet," I said quietly. "About her mom. Bash didn't tell her. CPS said their social worker would handle it."

Melissa closed her eyes for a moment. When she opened them, a tear trickled down her cheek. "I want to be there when they tell her."

"I'll ask, but I can't see why it would be a problem."

She looked toward the closed door where Evie was. "Will they let me keep her?"

"I honestly don't know. It'll depend on Bash and on Allison."

Her jaw tightened at Allison's name. "She's his mother." She said "his" like it was a cuss word.

"She's also Evie's grandmother. If she wants custody, it would be hard to argue she's not capable." I said it as gently as I could. "Where's Edgar?"

"Home." She smoothed her slacks. "He's better when he can be useful from a distance."

That tracked. Edgar Jones was a man built for the daily management of ordinary things. He wasn't cool under pressure, as I'd learned during the exploding kettle incident. Holding down the fort at home made sense for him. I didn't judge him for it. Some people weren't built for chaos.

"Let me see what I can find out." I patted her knee and got up to find Lance. As the only lawyer around, I hoped he might have some insight.

Lance had gone through to one of the side offices. I'd seen him head that way after Allison Green's phone call had sent him toward the exit for air. The door was half-open. I knocked once and pushed it the rest of the way.

He was at the desk, a laptop open in front of

him, looking at a paused image on the screen. He looked up, startled, when I walked in.

"Sorry," I said. "Didn't mean to sneak up on you."

"No, it's—" He straightened. "It's fine."

I sat down across the desk. "Melissa Jones. The aunt. She wants to know if she can keep Evie with her, at least temporarily. What are her chances? Realistically?"

He leaned back. "It's not impossible. But it depends on Bash and on Allison. If Allison decides she wants custody, she has the resources and the standing to make that complicated. The family relationship argument cuts both ways."

"Evie launched herself at Melissa like a heat-seeking missile the second she walked through the door," I said. "She barely reacted when Green came in. One of these things is not like the other."

"That matters in family court," he said. "But it doesn't decide things by itself."

I sat with the information for a moment. I looked at the corner of the desk and played Evie's game to settle my brain. Table. Gable. Clark. I looked at a handbag on a hook near the door. Bag. Drag. Trixxie Mattel.

Lance was watching me.

I looked at the laptop, then back at him. "Legal." I said it out loud without meaning to. "Smegal." And then in my best Gollum voice, very quietly, I hissed, "My precious."

Lance stared at me. "What?"

"Nothing. Just the game." I waved it off and stood up. "Thanks for the information for Melissa."

I headed for the door. My brain kept going. Legal. Eagle. Scout. Legal.

Beagle.

I stopped walking.

Legal. Beagle.

Snoopy is a beagle.

I stood in the doorway with my hand on the frame and the thought settled over me.

Could it be that simple? Snoopy was someone who deals with legal things. A cop. Or... I turned and looked back at Lance.

A lawyer.

My heart picked up the pace and I walked back into the office. Lance was at the laptop again, and now that I was looking, he wasn't watching the footage on the screen. His hands were moving on the keyboard.

"What are you doing?" I asked.

He looked up. His face had changed.

"Snoopy," I said. I watched his face.

I got my answer.

He shoved back from the desk and his hand went to his jacket pocket and came out with a gun. Seriously? I'd been taken hostage before, and I wasn't looking to do it again. I tried backing out of the room, but Lance shook the gun at me.

Great. Unhinged and no idea how to handle a weapon. "Just calm down," I told him, because those three words always did the trick.

"Come inside and close the door." His voice was shaking. "I have to do this. If I don't, she'll ruin me."

"Do what?"

"Erase the recording."

I narrowed my gaze. "For who?"

"Allison Green." His eyes went to the laptop screen. "She'll ruin my career and my marriage. She'll take everything if I don't do this."

I looked at the screen. The footage from Clive's Clippers. He wasn't watching it. He was trying to delete it.

"It doesn't matter," I said, more calmly than I felt. "That's a downloaded copy. The original is locked up in the evidence room." Truth. Broyles had put a copy on the server for Bash's interrogation, but the original drive was bagged and tagged. "You can erase this, but it's not going away."

His face fell as sweat beaded on his forehead. "It's too late anyway. Everyone will know." His voice cracked. "I can't go to jail. I can't—"

"Lance—"

"Don't." He steadied the gun and took a step toward me. "Be quiet. Don't make a fuss, and no one else gets hurt." His eyes moved toward the hallway, toward the room where Evie was, toward the chairs where Melissa sat. "Just help me get out of here, and I'll let you go."

"You can go now."

"Shut up," he snarled. He looked desperate to be anywhere else on earth. He might be Gerry's killer, but he was also clearly a man for whom none of this had ever been the plan. Even so, I wasn't about to argue with a loaded weapon. I walked back out into the hallway with Lance behind me, his hand at my back and the gun in his jacket pocket.

We passed Melissa. She looked up, and I tried to keep my face from saying anything useful to Lance. I didn't want to put her in danger. Unfortunately, Melissa was a smart cookie. Her eyes went sharp immediately, taking in Lance's posture, my posture, and the distance between us that wasn't right. She stayed put instead of doing something stupid, like calling someone Snoopy to see if they were a potential murderer.

We passed two uniformed officers who glanced up and went back to what they were doing.

Then Ezra came through the door from the interrogation hallway and stopped.

"Hey." He looked at me, then at Lance, then at the way Lance was standing. "What's going on?"

Lance pulled the gun out of his pocket and grabbed me by the shoulder and got the barrel against the side of my neck. I forced myself to breathe.

Across the station, Reese and Broyles had gone still. I caught Reese's eyes. Then Ezra's. I held them steady.

"I know you don't want to hurt anyone," I said. My voice was level. I was proud of it. "Gerry was a mistake. You didn't mean to hurt her."

Lance made a sound that wasn't quite a word. His grip on my shoulder tightened.

"I loved her," he said. His voice broke apart. "She didn't love me back. She wanted to leave. She was going to disappear and take everything with her, and I couldn't—" He stopped. "I couldn't let her go."

The pieces rearranged themselves in my head.

Lance scoring Gerry's pie. Lance knew her number. He'd told me he'd given it high marks. Tens across the board, or so I'd thought. He'd seemed to mean it.

But.

Oh.

Oh no.

Had he tanked her score to keep her from winning? Close enough that no one would question the scores. Far enough that she'd stay.

Melissa's voice came from somewhere behind me. She wasn't yelling. She was very clear and very steady.

"She needed that money for new identification," she said. "Birth certificates for her and Evie. She'd already paid a huge deposit, but she needed the last ten thousand before the forger would give her the documents. She was going to be free of Bash. She was going to take Evie and go somewhere safe."

"Shut up," Lance said. The gun moved off my neck and swung toward Melissa.

I felt Ezra's focus shift across the room. I didn't look at him. I didn't need to.

Reese had moved three feet closer. Broyles had moved five.

The front door opened.

Allison Green came through first, Shawn right

behind her, and Lance's head turned toward the door. The gun went with it.

I drove the heel of my shoe down onto the arch of his foot with everything I had.

He shouted. His grip on my shoulder loosened.

I slammed my head back. The crack of it against his chin was loud enough that I felt it in my back teeth, and then his hands were gone. I threw myself away from him as Reese and Broyles flew past me. They took Lance down, and the gun was knocked from his hand and skittered across the floor. It came to a stop against the baseboard, and a uniformed officer quickly scooped it up.

Ezra reached me in three steps. His hands were on my face, checking me over.

"I'm fine," I said. My heart was pounding. "I'm okay."

He exhaled.

"Ezra." I caught his wrist. "Lance is Snoopy. He's the one who killed Gerry."

Across the room, Reese had Lance face-down, cuffing his hands behind his back. She got up and read him his rights as Broyles lifted him to his feet. Shawn stood in the doorway with Allison Green beside him. The mayor looked shocked for a moment, then her expression went blank.

Evie's door was still closed.

That was the only thing I cared about right now. No one had gotten hurt, and that door was still closed.

MELISSA SAT across from Ezra in the small conference room off the main hallway, her hands folded on the table, and she told him everything as far as she knew.

"Gerry came to me a few months ago and told me that Bash had been physically abusing her since before Evie was born." She looked guilty and disgusted. "I couldn't believe it. I never knew. She always put on such a brave and happy face when we were together, which I'll admit hadn't been as much as I would've liked." She took a tissue and dabbed at her eyes. "Now I understand why. She was so scared of him, scared he was going to kill her, scared he would start hurting Evie." Melissa shook her head. "And she believed the police wouldn't help her. Bash repeatedly reminded her who his mother was." The grieving woman wrung her hands. "I'd given her thirty thousand dollars when she asked for it, because I wanted to help her, but it ran me short.

Edgar and I have a lot of assets, but not a lot of cash."

"Does Edgar know?" I asked. "What you were using the money for?"

"No," Melissa admitted. "I couldn't tell him that I was using our money to help Gerry get illegal documents, so I just let him believe what he wanted." She spread her hands. "That my niece was terrible with money and had racked up a large debt." Her hands became balled fists. "I spent close to two thousand dollars on fifty-fifty tickets — not all at once, spread out over weeks, small purchases here and there, nothing that would raise questions. I'd wanted to make sure the prize pool was high enough that Gerry's share would cover what she needed. I didn't tell Edgar where the money went. Instead, I filed it under household miscellaneous, which is the kind of accounting Edgar never looks too closely at."

"And Lance? What part did he play?"

"I knew Lance from fundraisers and other charitable events," she said. "I knew about the affair. Gerry told me." She looked at her hands. "When he ended things with Gerry, she'd been scared because he'd been helping her to leave Bash. She wouldn't tell me why he'd done it. Just that he had." She pressed her lips together. "I found out later that Allison Green had gone to him. Told him to end it or she'd tell his wife and make sure his career at the DA's office was finished."

Ezra didn't write anything down. He just listened.

"I was angry at him," Melissa said. "He'd promised to help Gerry. He'd said he loved her. And then the minute it got difficult, he walked away." She looked up. "So I called him. I told him I knew about the relationship, and I knew why he'd ended it, and I knew what his wife didn't. And I told him that if he didn't score Gerry's pie at the top, I would make sure Patricia Crabtree got a very detailed account of the last five months."

"Blackmail," Ezra said. Not a question.

"Yes." She didn't look away. "I know what it was. I know it was wrong. But for Gerry, I'd do it again."

LANCE WAS in a separate room with a public defender who had arrived in under an hour, which said something about how fast word traveled in Garden Cove. When Ezra and I went in, Lance was sitting with his elbows on the table and his face in his hands.

"I wasn't trying to kill her," he said, before Ezra had asked anything. "I want you to understand that. I went in there to talk to her. To make her see reason. My wife...Patricia had somehow found out and she was on the warpath. She'd already tried to confront Gerry before the pie contest."

Had that been who Gerry was avoiding? A scorned wife?

"And then you suffocated her," Ezra said.

Lance looked up. Surprise crossed his face at the statement, but he didn't argue. "I guess so," he admitted, then stared back at the table.

"She was already...she wasn't steady," he said. "From whatever happened earlier with Bash, obviously." He shook his head. "But I didn't know that. How could I? She said if I didn't give her the money, she'd tell Patricia everything. Everything. I couldn't. I had nothing left to give her. I'd already done what Melissa asked. I'd already scored the pie. And it still wasn't enough." His voice went flat. "She just kept pushing."

He didn't say anything else after that. The public defender put a hand on his arm.

Ezra closed his notebook.

Allison Green sat in Ezra's office with her ankles crossed and her hands in her lap, and she was very good at looking like a person in charge. Shawn was at the window. I was in the corner. What a weekend. So many revelations, but none of it felt settled to me.

"Whatever you think you saw Bash do, I can assure you—"

"We have clear footage of him," Ezra told her without uncertainty. "Your son."

Her voice was careful. "Which is a terrible thing."

"You knew he was hurting her," I said.

She looked at me. "I suspected, at times, that things were difficult between them."

"Difficult?" The woman was killed in a porta-potty because she was trying to get away from her dangerously abusive husband. I remembered the sharp chemical smell of the deodorizer, and how in her last fear-filled moments it was that scent that had solidified the memory.

I was angry when I stood up and left the office without explanation.

The janitor's closet was at the end of the hall. I opened it and looked around the shelves until I found what I needed, a small mesh pouch, bright blue, the same kind used in urinal cakes in every public restroom. The smell hit me when I picked it up, chemical and sharp and floral underneath, and I was back in the dark for just a moment before I steadied myself and walked back to the office.

"What is that?" Green said, when I came in.

"This was the last thing Gerry smelled when she died." I held it in front of her. "Your son is the reason this happened."

I didn't expect what happened next.

A woman moves quickly across the courthouse lawn, away from the grandstand, away from the crowd. The festival noise recedes behind her. She's dressed for the platform, blazer, heels, the green that reads well in photographs.

She watches a man in a linen jacket stagger out of the last portable toilet, bracing himself against the exterior, before moving away.

She slips inside.

Dark. She uses the flashlight on her phone, but the beam finds Gerry, crumpled forward on the seat.

"Geraldine?" she asks, checking for a pulse. A low moan from the crumpled woman shows she's still alive. Green puts her phone down, light still on.

She hesitates for only a moment before using both hands to cover the woman's face.

There is a soft sound. Then nothing.

She checks for a pulse again. Repositions the head. Takes toilet paper from the roll and wipes her hands, then the handle of the door, the wall, anything she might have touched. She stuffs it into her purse. Turns off the light on her phone. Opens the door a crack, checks, and steps out into the afternoon.

I was kneeling when the vision ended, and Ezra was beside me, his hand rubbing circles on my back. "Are you okay? What happened?"

Allison Green was watching me. She'd been mayor long enough to know about my gifts, and she was waiting to see what I had to say. Turns out, it was a lot.

"They all did it," I croaked. "Bash gave her the concussion. Lance overpowered her until she lost consciousness. And you walked in after Lance left and finished the job." The police station was full of monsters today.

"That's an extraordinary accusation," Green said. "And I'd like to know what possible proof you think you have. Do you think anyone is going to take the word of a charlatan over a beloved town leader?"

"You wouldn't be the first mayor of Garden Cove to be convicted of murder," Shawn said from the window.

Green looked at him. He glared back at her

before nodding at me. "Do you have a way to prove any of this?"

"Her purse," I said. "She used toilet paper to wipe down the stall. She stuffed it in her purse after." I looked at Green. "You also wiped the blood from Gerry's skull fracture off your hands with it."

She scoffed. "You're not going to find toilet paper in my purse."

"Maybe not," I told her. "But I'm willing to bet the forensics team finds blood and DNA transfer somewhere in the lining."

Allison Green's composure did not crack. But her eyes changed. For the first time since she'd walked into the room, she looked like a woman who understood that for the first time in her life she wasn't going to be able to campaign her way out of a mess.

CHAPTER
TWELVE

Two weeks later, Marco came home, and Gilly planned a welcome barbecue for him, which meant it was elaborate, well-stocked, and happening whether anyone was ready or not.

She'd strung lights across the back deck and set up two folding tables with checkered tablecloths, and the grill was Scott's domain, which he accepted with the focused pleasure of a man given a clear task and the right tools for it. Jordy and Pippa brought potato salad. Their kids were chasing each other around the yard, laughing and giggling like hyenas. Cute hyenas, but also a bit wild and feral.

Ezra was at the drinks table getting himself some punch. Gilly was everywhere at once, which was her natural state.

Marco sat in one of the deck chairs, and next to him was a young woman named Callie, who he'd brought home from college with him. She had dark eyes and an easy smile, but she also looked nervous as heck. I didn't blame her. Meeting the parents was always nerve-racking.

Ezra appeared at my elbow with two red plastic cups of sparkling punch. "You look beautiful," he said, in my ear.

"You say that every time."

"I mean it every time."

I leaned into him, enjoying the moment. The arrests made two weeks earlier had sent a rippling effect through town. Bart Lynde, the Mayor Pro Tem on the city council, had taken over for Green. Her son Bash had been charged with aggravated assault resulting in grievous bodily harm. The ME findings on Gerry's prior injuries resulted in additional charges. He was denied bail pending trial.

Lance Crabtree was arrested for accessory to murder, involuntary manslaughter under the state's felony murder provisions, criminal threatening, and unlawful possession of a firearm at a law enforcement facility. His attorney was trying to negotiate a deal, and his wife had emptied their bank accounts and left him.

Allison Green, the worst of the worst as far as I was concerned, was arrested for first-degree murder. She'd asked for a different attorney three times before settling on someone from Kansas City. The purse had come back from the forensics lab with Gerry's blood, skin cells, and even a hair in the lining. She had stopped making public statements. She was going down hard, and it couldn't happen to a more repulsive woman.

Rob Doyle was charged with bribery, fraud, and misuse of public office. Dora Charles had agreed to cooperate fully in exchange for reduced charges on the fraud and bribery counts. She'd already returned the prize money, which was being held pending resolution of the contest's legal status. I really hoped the money would go to Evie since Gerry would have won otherwise, but if I had to guess, third-place Sandy, the only untainted winner, would probably end up with the bounty.

Melissa's blackmail had never officially produced results, and Lance declined to press charges from his current address, which was a cell. The county awarded Melissa temporary guardianship of Evie, with the potential for adoption at six months if circumstances remained stable. I'd been there when Melissa got the call. I'd sat in the Joneses' family room with two Shih Tzus on my feet and watched Melissa's face go from rigid to undone as she inhaled the first real breath she'd taken in weeks.

Gerry had loved her daughter in every way she knew how, including the ones that were desperate and imperfect and ultimately too late. Melissa would do right by Evie. For Gerry, and for Gloria, and because Evie Green was seven years old and already knew how to find the bridge between things, and that wasn't a skill you wasted.

The lights in Gilly's yard were on and the air smelled like charcoal and late spring.

I thought about bridges. Chair to hair to wig. Legal to beagle to Snoopy. The threads we tie together without even knowing why sometimes.

"Hey." Ezra touched my arm. "You're somewhere else."

"No." I slipped into his arms. "I'm here. Right where I want to be."

Gilly called everyone to the table, and we filled plates and passed food around. Marco, who was always quiet, seemed even quieter as everyone else talked and laughed. Pippa was telling a story that made Tippi cover her mouth with both hands. Jordy poured more iced tea. Scott had his arm around Gilly's chair.

It was a good evening. The kind of evening that felt like the right side of things after the past couple of weeks.

Then Marco set down his fork.

"I need to tell everyone something," he said.

Gilly went still. I caught her expression and thought, briefly, a proposal, maybe?

"Mom." He looked at her. He looked at Callie. Then back at Gilly. "Callie and I got married last month." And with a quick rip of the Band-Aid, he added, "And we're going to have a baby."

The yard went very quiet. Even the crickets stopped chirping.

Then Pippa made a sound that was trying to be neutral and wasn't, and Tippi grabbed her arm, and Jordy cleared his throat. Ezra's hand found mine under the table. Marco married and a baby on the way hadn't been on my bingo card at all.

Gilly looked at her son. She looked at Callie. Scott kept his arm around her shoulder, waiting to see what she needed from him. She surprised us all by smiling as she declared, "We're having a baby!"

She stood up and went to Callie and put her arms around her. The young soon-to-be mom hugged her back. They were both crying. It made me cry, darn it.

Marco stood up and put his arms around both of them and the yard erupted with congratulations.

Later, after the plates were cleared and the kids were winding down and the men took over the backyard cleanup, Marco and his new bride had gone into town to see his friends and tell them the news. Pippa, Tippi, and I found Gilly at the far end of the deck, reclining on a lounge chair with a glass of sweet tea and her face turned up toward the string lights.

"Are you all right?" I asked.

She smiled. It was only a little sad. "I would've liked a wedding," she said. "I would've liked to see him in a suit and watch him look at her the way Scott looks at me." She set down her glass. "But life hands you what it hands you. And you can treat every surprise like a bomb, or you can treat it like a gift. I'm going to have a daughter-in-law and a grandchild. That's a gift. That's two gifts."

"Truth," Pippa agreed. "And let me say, I hope I grow up to be a mom like you. My kids will be all the luckier for it."

Tippi nudged her sister. "You're the best mom."

We all agreed she was great.

I sat down next to Gilly and put my arm around her shoulders. She leaned into me, the way she always had, since we were in elementary school and decided we were going to be friends. Best friends forever.

Ezra met my eyes from across the deck and his mouth curved, that small unhurried smile that was for me and me alone. When I'd come back to Garden Cove to care for my mom, I'd never meant for it to be a permanent move. I was going to go back to my corporate job until I retired. Thank heavens they'd made the decision to replace me. Staying in Garden Cove, building a business and a life with people I loved and who loved me back—that was truly a gift, and one I planned to never give up.

The End

What's next for Nora Black and her friends in Garden Cove?

Herbal Warning - Spring 2027

My name is Nora Black. I'm fifty-eight years old, and I know better than to stick my nose where it doesn't belong. I really do.

But when a new-to-Garden Cover herbalist is found dead at the soft opening of his holistic health shop, my scent-mojo determines a diagnosis of murder.

Now I'm sorting through memories as bitter as the victim's bad promises, along with a list of suspects with plenty of motive. Unfortunately, the killer knows exactly how to make murder look like a natural remedy.

YOU'VE GOT TAIL

PECULIAR MYSTERIES & ROMANCES BOOK 1

Chapter One

SOME PEOPLE JUMP into the deep end of the pool feet first, some head first, but I've always been a traditional belly-flopper. Splashy, messy, and usually painful. Which still didn't explain why I was sitting on the floor of a closed diner, nursing my bruised butt, not to mention my pride, and staring woefully at a naked unconscious man in the middle of Peculiar, Missouri.

My parents are crazy from way back. Maybe that's where I get it from. Seriously, who names a child Ambrosia Sunshine? Two hippies, that's who. They told me when I was old enough to resent the flower child name that they'd thought it was cool at the time, but I personally believe it was the result of one too many 'shrooms. As it is, I've been forced to sit through many painful renditions of "You Are My Sunshine." If I had a dead body for every time I was teased, well, let's just say I'd get an express pass to the electric chair. Although, if I got a sympathetic judge, he'd probably consider my lifetime served.

Maybe my parents' experimentation with drugs is what had made me psychic. (No, I didn't say psychotic. I said *psychic.*) On the other hand, it could also explain why I'm so bad at it.

My ability allows me glimpses, more like screenshots, of the past, present, and future. But, clearly, the visions have *not* been helpful over the years. And the side effects, sheesh. Most of the time I feel a little dizzy when they hit, but every once in a while, it's as if someone has taken a sledgehammer to the inside of my skull. Usually, I can feel one coming on; otherwise driving might be an issue. If only they made medic-alert bracelets for my type of ailment. It certainly hasn't been a gift.

That's why my friendship with Chavvah Trimmel is so important. We'd met at the community college in San Diego. She thought my name was weird and awesome all rolled up into a spring roll. After finding out her family's propensity for strange biblical names, I thought it was a bit of the pot calling the kettle rusty. Chavvah, or Chav, as she likes to be called, was my first best friend. And when she's around me, my psychic mojo kicks up twenty notches. It's as if I can tap into some kind of mystic hotline whenever she's near.

As a matter of fact, the last time I'd gotten a clear vision had been in my dining room back in California. Chav, who'd been renting my spare bedroom at the time, had just turned down the heat on the spaghetti sauce, and I was setting the table. We were having an "I finally dumped the cheating bastard" celebratory dinner. Did I mention I'm a bad psychic? So I hadn't a clue what I was walking in on when I caught my boyfriend of three years having sex with the skank waitress from the coffee shop. On my couch, no less. Jerk. I took his spare key and kicked his ass (and the couch) to the curb.

At dinner that night, when the vision hit me, I'd hit the ground, along with some clattering dishes. I saw a present moment of Chav's parents huddled together, debating whether to call her about her missing brother. Talk about being the bearer of bad news. I didn't blame her for not believing me at first, or the stunned look she gave me when she called her parents, and it turned out to be true. Her brother Judah had dropped off the map.

Chav flew back to Missouri the next day. After a year of searching for him, the local police had pretty much given up on Judah, but by that time, Chav had forgotten about the ocean and fallen in love with the little town of Peculiar. Hell, from her letters and phone calls, I'd kind of fallen in love with the place as well. She'd found a restaurant in the rural town, a real fixer-upper, for the two of us to run. A fifty-fifty partner split.

I wasn't supposed to leave California for another two weeks, and Chav had said she needed to talk to me "in person" before I made the trip, but the text I'd gotten from her had sent me packing in a hurry.

All it said was: *Sunny. I need u.*

After that, every call I'd made to Chav went straight to voice mail. Without any real plan, I jumped into my gas-guzzling Toyota 4X4, which I had purchased explicitly for the move. One thousand six hundred and sixty-two point four miles later, as I drove over a swinging bridge (the only way in and out, I soon discovered) into the quaint little town, my whole body heaved a sigh of relief. I felt strangely wonderful. It was as if someone unzipped my off-the-rack skin and fitted me with a tailored Sunny suit.

The town looked very similar to Mayberry from *The Andy Griffith Show*. Dirt streets, old fashioned shops and houses, white picket fences, and lots of Chevy and Ford pickup trucks. I was a little nervous when my GPS said, "You have arrived," right outside a two-story yellow building on the corner of Third Street and Main.

My heart pounded as I stood outside our restaurant for the first time. I'd always expected some kind of fanfare. Chav waiting to usher me into our future. She'd even named the restaurant for me. Sunny's Outlook. I'd blame allergies for my eyes watering at that moment, but I knew it was a mixture of happiness and sadness all rolled into one big bundle. This was *our* place. Mine and Chav's. And she'd done it up spectacularly.

I smiled at the brightly colored lettering. All the letters except the big O in Outlook were blue. The O was not an O at all, but a bright orange sun. If it was possible to feel both warm and cold at the same time, I accomplished it.

Where was Chav? I knew in my bones something was wrong. The year we'd spent apart had dulled my psychic ability toward her, so once again I had become inept with crazy flashes that didn't amount to much of anything.

I jiggled the door handle. It wasn't locked, so being the smart, city-savvy girl I am, I decided to let myself in. After all, I owned half the joint, so I wasn't trespassing.

Darkness enclosed the front room except a few areas illuminated by sunlight filtering into the two small windows near the ceiling. They were surrounded by open wooden shutters. Where were the large storefront windows? This place was more dive bar than restaurant. Strange decor choice but my concern for Chav kept me from imagining a complete makeover. I couldn't find a light switch around the door. I should have just gone back out to the truck for a flashlight, but I thought I saw a panel on the wall across the room, and frankly, it was sheer laziness that moved me forward.

I managed to maneuver around the counter, open the panel, and flicked several of the switches at once. The lights came on and when I stepped back to admire my new home lit up—it didn't look half bad; hardwood floors, cute little tables with black-and-white gingham cloth, and a couple of booths with the same checkered design on the benches.

And that's when it happened. My heel caught on something large, and I fell ass-backward to the ground. It didn't take more than a nanosecond to see that I'd tripped over a naked man passed out cold on the floor.

After a startled yelp, heart palpitations, and worry that he'd wake up at any moment and kill me, I reached over and touched him. Just his arm, mind you. He didn't move, but his skin felt warm, and his chest raised and lowered, so I didn't bother to check for a pulse.

Instead, I found myself staring...for several minutes. (Come on. He was naked and lying on his back. Who wouldn't stare?) Dark-brown hair populated his broad chest and led to a happy trail that, well, if the circumstances had been different would have made me very happy indeed. He had thickly muscled thighs and arms, and his face, except for the scruffy five o'clock shadow, looked as if it had been chiseled by Michelangelo. Imagine a better-looking Wolverine (Hugh Jackman's version), but much younger and with a burly lumberjack vibe, and coarse, medium-length walnut-brown hair.

I chewed my lower lip as I took my time pondering the situation—in other words, I wasn't ready to stop staring at the naked man. His hair was near the same hue of brown as my own, when it wasn't dyed blonde, which was never. And mine was shorter with a better haircut. I sighed with regret. I already missed my stylist in California.

Taking a deep breath, I counted backward from ten to pull myself out of the hormonal frenzy going on in my head. The man was hotter than a habanero, but I wasn't looking for a date. I smelled a pungent sweet scent I hadn't noticed before, but frankly I was surprised any of my senses still worked. It was whiskey. Some kind of blended version, if I had to guess.

Great. Just perfect. Burly Hugh looked more and more like a drunk who had crawled into the diner to sleep off a bender.

I found an empty spray bottle by the sink and filled it with water. Positioning myself on the opposite side of the checkout counter (just in case I needed to make a run for it), I leaned over the top and proceeded to spritz the unconscious man. The mist must have been too fine, because other than the rise and fall of his chest, he still didn't move.

Crawling farther up onto the counter, I stretched my arms over the other side, hovering just inches from his face. I pumped the trigger hard three or four times, then screamed and dropped the bottle when his hand shot up and grabbed my wrist. The Neanderthal yanked me completely over the top and onto his naked self. He growled— honest to goodness, I wouldn't lie about such a thing. He growled. The noise started in his chest. I know, because I could feel it in mine, which was now crushed against him.

Why hadn't I just left and called the police? It would have been the easy thing to do—the smart thing. His arms were squeezed tight around me, and I became acutely aware of his Mr. Happy pressing against the skin of my thigh.

His eyelids cracked a peep, then he narrowed his gaze. "Who are you?"

"I..." I should be the one asking the damn questions, but the only ones coming to mind were completely inappropriate. Like, where did he work out? How good looking were his parents to create such a fine specimen of man? And did he have a girlfriend?

There was a moment, a very weak moment on my part, where I began to lower my face to his, our lips only centimeters apart.

What the hell am I doing? Where was my head? He could be a serial killer, a rapist, or someone *really* bad, like an Amway salesman. I turned my head away from his.

"Could you let me up, please?"

He squeezed me tighter. "Are you going to answer me?"

Finally, I gulped and squeaked out, "Sunny Haddock."

His left eyebrow rose. "Sunny Haddock?"

"Uh, that would be me. Yes." I'd been in town less than an hour and I was already famous. Well, my name was on the side of the building. "And you would be?"

"Babel Trimmel."

"Chav's baby brother?" I'd heard stories about him, but I'd imagined him to be terminally twelve. The age he'd been when Chav had left Missouri for the West Coast.

"Chavvie made a big mistake. She shouldn't have asked you out here."

Talk about judging someone before you get the know them. Barely through introductions and he already wanted me out. I've made a bad first impression before, but what the fuck? What didn't he like about me? Although maybe it wasn't about like. Because, by the rise of his hoo-ha against my leg, I could swear he liked me a little.

An unfamiliar flutter twittered in my stomach. It'd been awhile since I'd been so physically attracted to anyone. Babel's nostrils flared with a slight huff. His brows narrowed. His eyes dark with purpose. I felt like Little Red Riding Hood, and Babel filled the role of the Big Bad Wolf intent on eating my goody basket. Oh, if only.

Pull yourself together, Sunny. But it was really hard, along with his arms, his chest, his abs, his...

Holding me tighter, his arms locked around me. He stroked my back with his firm hands. I trembled, fighting back a deep moan. "Please let me up, Babel," I said again.

He froze for a second then relaxed. He unlocked his arms from around me and smiled. "Call me Babe. Everybody does."

To say I scrambled off his body would be a bit of an overstatement. The trembling had left my arms and knees weak, but I managed, albeit slowly. "I don't know you well enough to call you Babe. Sorry." I couldn't keep my eyes off his semi-erect package.

"Could you put some clothes on? I'm feeling a little..."

He propped up on an elbow like a *Playgirl* centerfold and grinned. "Overdressed?"

What an egomaniac! "No. Sheesh." Okay, so maybe

I felt a tad overdressed, even in my pink spaghetti-strap shirt dress with black short-shorts and sandals. It was hot in Missouri. Sticky hot. And besides, I'd put in more hours than I care to count at the gym to counterbalance my donut habit, so I deserved to wear those shorts. My exercise routine wasn't all about the donuts. Over a year of no sex, since the dickhead had cheated, and while I'm no sex maniac, that's a long time for someone who had been getting it on the reg.

The "no sex" could also explain why I had such a visceral reaction to this guy. No doubt the man was a hunka-hunka. "Could you quit posing on the floor?" I wagged my finger toward his poker. "And for the love of daisies, put some clothes on before that thing puts out someone's eye."

He had the courtesy to look the tiniest bit embarrassed. "Nothing personal. It's a purely physical reaction."

"I'm sure you say that to all the girls."

"Sorry, I just meant, well, I'm a guy. You brush against the junk, it goes stiff."

"And here I thought I was special." This line of conversation bordered on hurting my feelings. I know I'm not a beauty queen, but neither am I Medusa. "You can shut up now."

Color rose to his cheeks—those nice fuzzy, chiseled, scruffy, manly cheeks, so perfectly bookending his Roman nose and gorgeous bow lips. And damn it to hell, his teeth were friggin' perfect! He pulled himself up by grabbing the counter, and holy schmoly, the man was tall. If I had to guess, he bordered on 6'5". I'm pretty sure I hated him for being so beautifully handsome.

"I only meant to say..."

I almost offered to buy him a shovel, but he managed to dig his own hole quite deep without any help from me. "I've got it already, jeesh. Not interested, physical reaction, yadda, yadda, yadda. No need to explain yourself further. Besides, I'm not looking for a boyfriend, so doesn't matter. And even if I were, it certainly wouldn't be my best friend's baby brother. We cool?" I didn't wait for him to answer. I waved him off. "Great. Excellent. Awesome even. Now, put on some damn clothes." Why-oh-why was I attracted to crazy?

"Perhaps you could find me a diaper."

Guess he didn't like the "baby" comment. Oh well. Sucks to be him.

He covered himself with his hands. Thank God. However, it didn't stop me from checking out the rest of his body. *Ay Chihuahua!* Damn, it kind of sucked to be me.

I knew from Chav that Babel had moved back to Kansas City where their parents lived after he'd taken a year off from university to look for their brother Judah. What was he still doing here? A horrible thought entered my head. "If you're here, does that mean..."

His face suddenly sobered. "I don't know. Mom and Dad haven't been able to get ahold of her for the last couple of days, so they sent me down to check in. I got here yesterday."

"She texted me a couple of days ago. I haven't been able to get ahold of her since then." I lifted a hand to comfort him, but his nakedness stopped me from breaching the distance. "Babel, we're going to find her." Even if I had to turn over every stump and stone in this backward-ass town.

"Call me Babe. Everyone does."

That was the second time he'd said that to me, but I couldn't call him Babe. No way, no how. Too intimate. Especially since I'd seen him in his birthday suit. "I don't think so."

He chuckled, low and sexy, and everything went right south of my navel. "Sunny,

I'm afraid I've, err...lost my clothes."

"You've got to be kidding me." How did a person go about losing all their damn clothes? "Fine. I'll stay on one side of the counter. You stay on the other. Kapeesh?"

"I understand," he said with a practiced tolerance. It made me wonder who he'd gotten so much practice with.

He hadn't turned around yet, and part of me felt really sad about it. I'm sure he had a killer butt to go with his killer bod. I was all about the teeth and ass. But there were no complaints about the whole frontal part of him either, so...

"Good. Should I call someone for you? Or do you want to call someone? A girlfriend? Anyone who can bring you some clothes?" Subtle. Not.

"The phone's not working here even if I could call someone."

I noticed he'd didn't say "no girlfriend." Much to my annoyance, I cared. And why was the phone turned off? "Don't you have a cell phone that works?"

He moved his hands, indicating his lack of attire. "No pockets."

In the immortal words of Homer Simpson, *Doh*! I snuck another quick glance at his dangly bits, even more annoyed with myself for not having better self-control. "Great. Fantastic." I waved my hand again and purposefully looked away. I had a cell phone out in my truck, and was just about to tell him I'd go get it when he stepped out from behind the counter, still full Monty. "Hey! Keep the mammoth covered."

"Flattering. But there's nothing prehistoric about it." He cocked his eyebrow and smirked.

Bastard.

"Look here, darling." He pointed to his "junk" as he'd called it and said, "This here is what you call a penis. It's connected to the bladder and the bladder is full. Turn your head if you want, sweetheart, but I'm heading to the john."

"Lovely. And I'm not your darling." I made a show of rolling my eyes and turning away. "I'm going to get my cell phone. I expect you to be standing behind the counter by the time I get back." Now, for the sake of posterity—well, at least for the sake of his posterior—I glanced back as he headed left to the bathroom. Of course, it was sort of hard to notice his ass when I saw the— "Blood..." I whispered.

A pain pierced my temple as my knees buckled beneath me. I dropped to the ground. My peripheral vision narrowed to black. The pounding of blood racing through my arteries swelled loudly in my ears. It was out of beat with my heart.

The thumping of blood stopped, my eyesight began to clear, and I was in Babel's arms.

"Sunny? You okay?" I heard his voice as a muffled echo.

No, I wanted to tell him. I wasn't okay. But my mouth didn't work. A vision came over me. I could sense it like death come knocking. Then I was no longer in Babel's arms. I was a ghost. A spectator.

I was...in a shabby apartment with furniture dating back to the seventies? Had I traveled to the past? It wasn't unheard of for me, but it couldn't be relevant for something in my life now since I hadn't been born until 1974. Or could it? Great. The powers that be were giving me a psychic reading on my lost Crissy doll. Useless.

I heard a muffled cry, maybe a scream from beyond the front door. I passed through and down the stairs. The noise grew louder. Animalistic growls and snarls. Fear tightened in my stomach.

It's not real, I reminded myself several times as the feral sounds made me shiver.

I couldn't see any creature, but it certainly sounded like someone was getting voraciously attacked. And the room—it looked familiar. Two windows high up on the far wall spilled moonlight across the floor to...the counter? This was the restaurant. The noise continued, loud, animalistic, with grunting, groaning, and a masculine "ah!" Oh. Oh no.

If I'd really been there, I'd have run, but the vision took me closer to the scene of the crime. On the floor, behind the counter, a gorgeous woman with long dark hair, golden eyes, and even in the bad lighting, a body I'd give my right tit for, straddled the very naked and very sexy Babel Trimmel. I wanted to gouge out my eyes. Where was a hot poker salesman when you needed him?

The woman threw her head back and laughed. "You were fantastic, Babe. As always."

He smiled, his eyes rolling back a little. Coming up on his elbows, he leaned his left shoulder forward and looked behind. "You've got to do something about those fingernails."

"Just marking my territory."

Holy smack, the blood on the floor had happened during sexcapades? Yikes.

"I'm not your territory, Sheila."

The woman, Sheila apparently, picked up a bottle of Canadian Mist from the floor beside them, took a swig, then dumped some of the amber liquid down his large chest. No wonder the place reeked.

Babel shook his head and gave her thigh a light slap.

"It's time to go, Sheila. I've got to get the place cleaned up."

"You sure you don't want to move here?" She licked his nipple. "I've sure missed you."

He sighed. The sigh sounded like it'd been one that he'd perfected over and over for this very argument. "It's not this town or you. I've got a real life out there.*" He said "there" as though he was talking about an alien planet. "I'm going to find my sister, then get back to it."*

"And what if you don't find her?" Sheila asked. "You never found Judah."

Babel's eyes narrowed. "Not an option," he said. Then added, "I'm finding her, and after, getting the heck out of this town. It's brought nothing but bad luck for my family."

"Sorry," she said, as if she wasn't sorry, an evil smile playing on her lips. Okay, so maybe more mischievous than evil, but it was my vision, I could use whatever adjectives I liked. "But you know that answer pisses me off."

Before he could blink, she whacked him super hard across the temple with the bottle of blended whiskey, and Babel was out like a light.

"Bastard," Sheila muttered. Which I understood, because it had been my sentiment exactly.

She dressed quickly, gathered up Babel's clothes, and

walked into the kitchen area. It was small, but nice. I hadn't had a chance to see it yet, so it was like my very own psychic tour. She opened the walk-in freezer and chucked the jeans, boots, socks, and T-shirt inside. No underwear. Huh. I'd file that nugget away for later.

My vision stopped with her slamming the front door, and suddenly I was back, looking up from the floor at the towering and still very naked Babel. "Ow." My head, my back, my butt—everything hurt. "Did you drop me?"

"What the hell just happened?" He looked a little freaked out.

I got up on my elbows and rubbed the back of my skull. "Did you drop me on the ground?"

"You were having a seizure or something. I laid you on the floor." He was definitely freaked. "If I'd had a phone I'd have called for the doc, but..."

"I'm fine now. You can stop worrying." I moved my feet off the chair Babel had propped them up on. "I'm sorry. I'm squeamish about blood."

Which wasn't a complete lie. Blood tended to bring on funky psychic mojo that left me drained and pained. Although, I'll admit, these visions had been much stronger than normal. Apparently, Chavvah wasn't the only Trimmel who put my psychic stuff on speed dial.

"I'm getting that about you." At least he sounded less upset.

I closed my eyes. "Why would you let someone do that to your back?"

"That's a story for another day, darlin'."

Yeah, I knew the story. Not so sure I wanted the blow-by-blow again. I felt his arms go under me, and I opened my eyes, staring into the deep abyss of his gorgeous, Midwest baby blues.

I let him carry me upstairs to the apartment. I'm not a small woman, but he held me like I weighed next to nothing, which made me think kindlier of him. With my arms around his shoulders, I could smell an unidentifiable musk and spice to his skin. He sat me down on a couch—the scent went from musky to musty—then he went into another room. I heard water running in the sink. More than a whisper of regret passed through me. I barely knew the man and I missed being in his arms. I looked around the living room.

This was the seventies place where my vision had started. The retro decor lacked any sophistication that could've made the space sensational. I knew this had been where Judah lived when he'd been in town. He'd rented this building before his disappearance, and Chav had used our stake to purchase it during her search for him. His vanishing had hit her hard.

Chav told me once that she hadn't agreed with her oldest brother's "lifestyle choice," but she respected him. I'd asked her what she meant, but she had shaken her head, unwilling to elaborate. I knew it wasn't as simple as him being gay or anything like that, because Chav, like myself, was socially liberal. Hell, she'd have started her own PFLAG (Parents, Families, and Friends of Lesbians and Gays) in Peculiar if that had been the case. No. There was something else she hadn't approved of.

I heard the water turn off in the kitchen. Babel returned and proceeded to wipe my face and neck with a cool cloth.

"There now, all better." For a second, he sounded like my father. Which totally squicked me, considering the hard-core fantasies I had about him. He put the washcloth in my hand and patted my shoulder. "I'm going to jump in the shower real quick. I'll be back in a few."

Part of me wanted to watch him walk away strictly for the view, but since that part seemed to have done gone and lost its damn mind, I waited until I heard water running before looking in his direction.

He'd left the bathroom door open. Perv.

I couldn't believe it, less than an hour in a new town and I'd witnessed a *Red Shoe Diary* moment, and the star was lathering up less than ten feet away. I would've been downright disgusted by the whole morning if I hadn't been so preoccupied with thoughts of slippery suds sliding along his perfectly formed pecs. (Now I understand how bad porn gets started. Bow chick-a bow-wow.)

I will not go stare at the naked man. I repeated this mantra in my head over and over as I ran down the stairs to the kitchen.

Grabbing his clothes from the freezer, I contemplated where they'd been and how they got there as I carried them back upstairs. They were cold and held the scent of sweat, but at least he'd have something to put on so he could go away. I placed them on the couch, and dear Lord, it was a really ugly couch. It would be the first piece of furniture to go when Chav and I started fixing the place up. And with that thought, I went downstairs to wait for him.

Fifteen minutes later, the light flickered on in the stairwell. Babel's arms and face glistened with dewy goodness as he walked down the steps. He rubbed a tea towel, barely big enough to dry a fish's butt, against his loose mane of wet hair. His blue T-shirt clung to his chest. Water soaking through the fabric made spots the color of midnight.

He must have felt me staring, because he dropped his arm to his side and looked at me. "Where'd you find my clothes?"

"The freezer." I wrapped my knuckle on the counter. "Guess you can go home now."

"Guess so." He shrugged as he stretched his body to tuck in his shirt. "But we should probably talk."

"I'm in no mood." *For talk.* Damn, he was superfine.

"Well, you kind of need to get in the mood." He shook his hair out, droplets spraying out around him. It began to feel like a bad (or really good, depending on who you asked) shampoo commercial. "There's been a mistake. My sister should've never invited you out here, Sunny."

"You've said that already, but unfortunately for you, my name's on the property, same as hers, all legal and binding. I'm staying. Period. End of discussion. Besides, I'm not going anywhere until I find Chav."

Babel chewed his lower lip and narrowed his eyes at me. "I don't think you understand the situation."

"Oh, I think I do. You don't like me. Fine. I get that."

"It's a might more complicated than that." He scratched at his five o'clock shadow.

I resisted the temptation to offer him a hand. "Why do you care, anyway? Don't you have a *real* life you want to get back to? You seem awfully concerned for a guy who isn't even sticking around."

"And what makes you think that?" Babel asked.

"Uh..." Fair question. I couldn't exactly tell him that I'd heard him tell his cuh-razy lover in a vision. "Well, you didn't exactly stick around after the search was called off for Judah."

A pained expression crossed his face. I instantly regretted being such an ass. It was a low blow, and petty even.

"I stayed for as long as I could stand it." He shook his head. "I'm not meant for this place, Sunny. And neither are you."

Another twinge. "It doesn't matter." We would find Chavvah, then he would be gone. "Have you heard anything? Are the police searching for her?"

"No and yes. I haven't heard from Chavvie, but Sheriff Taylor isn't giving up." He flicked his thumb-nail against his ring fingernail. "Not yet, anyways."

"She'll show up, Babel. I just know it." But I

didn't know it. In my heart, I believed she was alive, and not because of any vision. "She's my best friend. I'd feel it if she was gone. Now, go on back to wherever you're staying..." Oh, crap. Maybe he'd been staying here. "You do have another place to stay don't you?"

Babel nodded once. "I've been staying at Chavvie's cabin down by the lake."

"Good," I whispered. I'd want to check out her place later for clues to what happened. "It's been a long drive for me, and I need a nap so I can figure out what I have to do next to find her."

He shook his head as if he was having an argument with himself. "I'll be back in a couple of hours with some cleaning supplies and get the floor behind the counter scrubbed."

I didn't want to talk anymore. I wanted to get my bags out of the truck. I'd hassle with unpacking the U-Haul later, but the bags were a must. I needed something personal, something of mine in this place. I held out my hand. "That's a nice offer. I can manage. Thanks."

Babel took my hand, and gave me a tight-lipped smile. "You don't handle blood very well. After I clean it up, maybe we can compare notes about Chavvie."

I nodded, afraid that if I spoke the dams would open and I wouldn't be able to stop the tears. Then I heard a voice like a whisper in my ear.

Save her.

Babel let go of my hand. "I'll be back." The way he said it sounded more like a threat than a promise. As he walked out the front door, he added, "You've got an audience."

Get this book from your favorite eTailer!

PIT PERFECT MURDER

BARKSIDE OF THE MOON COZY MYSTERIES BOOK 1

Chapter 1 - Sneak Peek

When I was eighteen years old, I came home from a sleepover and found my mom and dad with their throats cut, and their hearts ripped from their chests.

My little brother Danny was in a broom closet in the kitchen, his arms wrapped around his knees, and his face pale and ghostly. Until that day, I'd planned to go to college and study medicine after graduation, but instead, I ended up staying home and taking care of my seven-year-old brother.

Seventeen years later, my brother was murdered. At the time, Danny's death looked like it would go unsolved, much like my parents' had.

Without Haze Kinsey, my best friend since we

were five, the killers would have gotten away with it. She was a special agent for the FBI for almost a decade, and when I called her about Danny's death, she dropped everything to come help me get him justice. The evil group of witches and Shifters responsible for the decimation of my family paid with their lives.

Yes. I said witches and Shifters. Did I forget to mention I'm a werecougar? Oh, and my friend Hazel is a witch. Recently, I discovered witches in my own family tree on my mother's side. Shifters, in general, only mated with Shifters, but witches were the exception. As a matter of fact, my friend Haze is mated to a bear Shifter.

I wouldn't have known about the witch in my genealogy, though, if a rogue witch coven hadn't done some funky hoodoo witchery to me. Apparently, the spell activated a latent talent that had been dormant in my hybrid genes.

My ancestor's magic acted like truth serum to anyone who came near her. No one could lie in her presence. Lucky me, my ability was a much lesser form of hers. People didn't have to tell me the truth, but whenever they were around me, they had the compulsion to overshare all sorts of private matters about themselves. This can get seriously uncomfortable for all parties involved. Like, the fact that I didn't need to know that Janet Strickland had been wearing the same pair of underwear for an entire week, or that Mike Dandridge had sexual fantasies about clowns.

My newfound talent made me unpopular and unwelcome in a town full of paranormal creatures who thrived on little deceptions. So, when Haze discovered the whereabouts of my dad's brother, a guy I hadn't known even existed, I sold all my belongings, let the bank have my parents' house, jumped in my truck, and headed south.

After two days and 700 miles of nonstop gray, snowy weather, I pulled my screeching green and yellow mini-truck into an auto repair shop called The Rusty Wrench. Much like my beloved pickup, I'd needed a new start, and moving to a small town occupied by humans seemed the best shot. I'd barely made it to Moonrise, Missouri before my truck began its death throes. The vehicle protested the last 127 miles by sputtering to a halt as I rolled her into the closest spot.

The shop was a small white-brick building with a one-car garage off to the right side. A black SUV and a white compact car occupied two of the six parking spots.

A sign on the office door said: *No Credit Cards. Cash Only. Some Local Checks Accepted (Except from Earl—You Know Why, Earl! You check-bouncing bastard).*

A man in stained coveralls, wiping a greasy tool with a rag, came out the side door of the garage. He had a full head of wavy gray hair, bushy eyebrows over light blue, almost colorless eyes, and a minimally lined face that made me wonder about his age. I got out of the truck to greet him.

"Can I help you, miss?" His voice was soft and raspy with a strong accent that was not quite Deep South.

"Yes, please." I adjusted my puffy winter coat. "The heater stopped working first. Then the truck started jerking for the last fifty miles or so."

He scratched his stubbly chin. "You could have thrown a rod, sheared the distributor, or you have a bad ignition module. That's pretty common on these trucks."

I blinked at him. I could name every muscle in the human body and twelve different kinds of viruses, but I didn't know a spark plug from a radiator cap. "And that all means..."

"If you threw a rod, the engine is toast. You'll need a new vehicle."

"Crap." I grimaced. "What if it's the other thingies?"

The scruffy mechanic shrugged. "A sheared distributor is an easy fix, but I have to order in the part, which means it won't get fixed for a couple of days. Best-case scenario, it's the ignition module. I have a few on hand. Could get you going in a couple of hours, but..." he looked over my shoulder at the truck and shook his head, "...I wouldn't get your hopes up."

I must've looked really forlorn because the guy said, "It might not need any parts. Let me take a look at it first. You can grab a cup of coffee across the street at Langdon's One-Stop."

He pointed to the gas station across the road. It didn't look like much. The pale-blue paint on the front of the building looked in need of a new coat, and the weather-beaten sign with the store's name on it had seen better days. There was a car at the gas pumps and a couple more in the parking lot, but not enough to call it busy.

I'd had enough of one-stops, though, thank you. The bathrooms had been horrible enough to make a wereraccoon yark, and it took a lot to make those garbage eaters sick. Besides, I wasn't just passing through Moonrise, Missouri.

"Have you ever heard of The Cat's Meow Café?" Saying the name out loud made me smile the way it had when Hazel had first said it to me. I'd followed my GPS into town, so I knew I wasn't too far away from the place.

"Just up the street about two blocks, take a right on Sterling Street. You can't miss it. I should have some news in about an hour or so, but take your time."

"Thank you, Mister..."

"Greer." He shoved the tool in his pocket. "Greer Knowles."

"I'm Lily Mason."

"Nice to meet ya," said Greer. "The place gets hoppin' around noon. That's when church lets out."

I looked at my phone. It was a little before noon now. "Good. I could go for something to eat. How are the burgers?"

"Best in town," he quipped.

I laughed. "Good enough."

Even in the sub-freezing temperature, my hands were sweating in my mittens. I wasn't sure what had me more nervous, leaving the town I grew up in for the first time in my life or meeting an uncle I'd never known existed.

I crossed a four-way intersection. One of the

signs was missing, and I saw the four-by-four post had snapped off at its base. I hadn't noticed it on my way in. Crap. Had I run a stop sign? I walked the two blocks to Sterling. The diner was just where Greer had said. A blue truck, a green mini-coup, and a sheriff's SUV were parked out front.

An alarm dinged as the glass door opened to The Cat's Meow. Inside, there was a row of six booths along the wall, four tables that seated four out in the open floor, and counter seating with about eight cushioned black stools. The interior décor was rustic country with orange tabby kitsch everywhere. A man in blue jeans and a button-down shirt with a string tie sat in the nearest booth. A female police officer sat at a counter chair sipping coffee and eating a cinnamon roll. Two elderly women, one with snowball-white hair, the other a dyed strawberry-blonde, sat in a back booth.

The white poof-headed lady said, "This egg is not over-medium."

"Well, call the mayor," said Redhead. "You're unhappy with your eggs. Again."

"See this?" She pointed at the offending egg. "Slime, right here. Egg snot. You want to eat it?"

"If it'll make you shut up about breakfast food, I'll eat it and lick the plate."

A man with copper-colored hair and a thick beard, tall and well-muscled, stepped out of the kitchen. He wore a white apron around his waist, and he had on a black T-shirt and blue jeans. He held a plate with a single fried egg shining in the middle.

The old woman with the snowy hair blushed, her thin skin pinking up as he crossed the room to their table. "Here you go, Opal. Sorry 'bout the mix-up on your egg." He slid the plate in front of her. "This one is pure perfection." He grinned, his broad smile shining. "Just like you." He winked.

Opal giggled.

The redhead rolled her eyes. "You're as easy as the eggs."

"Oh, Pearl. You're just mad he didn't flirt with you."

As the women bickered over the definition of flirting, the cook glanced at me. He seemed startled to see me there. "You can sit anywhere," he said. "Just pick an open spot."

"I'm actually looking for someone," I told him.

"Who?"

"Daniel Mason." Saying his name gave me a hollow ache. My parents had named my brother

Daniel, which told me my dad had loved his brother, even if he didn't speak about him.

The man's brows rose. "And why are you looking for him?"

I immediately knew he was a werecougar like me. The scent was the first clue, and his eyes glowing, just for a second, was another. "You're Daniel Mason, aren't you?"

He moved in closer to me and whispered barely audibly, but with my Shifter senses, I heard him loud and clear. "I go by Buzz these days."

"Who's your new friend, Buzz?" the policewoman asked. Now that she was looking up from her newspaper, I could see she was young.

He flashed a charming smile her way. "Never you mind, Nadine." He gestured to a waitress, a middle-aged woman with sandy-colored hair, wearing a black T-shirt and a blue jean skirt. "Top off her coffee, Freda. Get Nadine's mind on something other than me."

"That'll be a tough 'un, Buzz." Freda laughed. "I don't think Deputy Booth comes here for the cooking."

"More like the cook," the elderly lady with the light strawberry-blonde hair said. She and her friend cackled.

The policewoman's cheeks turned a shade of crimson that flattered her chestnut-brown hair and pale complexion. "Y'all mind your P's and Q's."

Buzz chuckled and shook his head. He turned his attention back to me. "Why is a pretty young thing like you interested in plain ol' me?"

I detected a slight apprehension in his voice.

"If you're Buzz Mason, I'm Lily Mason, and you're my uncle."

The man narrowed his dark-emerald gaze at me. "I think we'd better talk in private."

Keep Reading!

PARANORMAL MYSTERIES & ROMANCES

BY RENEE GEORGE

Nora Black Midlife Psychic Mysteries

Sense & Scent Ability (Book 1)

For Whom the Smell Tolls (Book 2)

War of the Noses (Book 3)

Aroma With A View (Book 4)

Spice and Prejudice (Book 5)

Age of Inno-Scents (Book 6)

Aroma Holiday (Book 7)

Vapes of Wrath (Book 8)

The Scented Cipher (Book 9)

Of Spice and Men (Book 10)

Lime and Punishment (Book 11)

Grimoires of a Middle-aged Witch

Earth Spells Are Easy (Book 1)

Spell On Fire (Book 2)
When the Spells Blows (Book 3)
Spell Over Troubled Water (Book 4)
Ghost in the Spell (Book 5)

Destiny of a Middle-aged Witch

Burning Djinn of Fire (Book 1)
Djinn Bottle Blues (Book 2)
Stand By Your Djinn (Book 3)

Peculiar Mysteries & Romances

You've Got Tail (Book 1)
My Furry Valentine (Book 2)
Thank You For Not Shifting (Book 3)
My Hairy Halloween (Book 4)
In the Midnight Howl (Book 5)
Furred Lines (Book 6)
My Wolfy Wedding (Book 7)
Who Let The Wolves Out? (Book 8)
My Thanksgiving Faux Paw (Book 9)
You Can't Furry Love (Book 10)

Witchin' Impossible Paranormal Mysteries

Witchin' Impossible (Book 1)
Rogue Coven (Book 2)
Familiar Protocol (Booke 3)

Mr & Mrs. Shift (Book 4)

FurOut (Book 5)

Barkside of the Moon Paranormal Mysteries

Pit Perfect Murder (Book 1)

Murder & The Money Pit (Book 2)

The Pit List Murders (Book 3)

Pit & Miss Murder (Book 4)

The Prune Pit Murder (Book 5)

Two Pits and A Little Murder (Book 6)

Pits and Pieces of Murder (Book 7)

Pittie Party Murder (Book 8)

A Wedding Pit-astrophy (Book 9)

Hex Drive

Hex Me, Baby, One More Time (Book 1)

Oops, I Hexed It Again (Book 2)

I Want Your Hex (Book 3)

Hex Me With Your Best Shot (Book 4)

Hex Me All Night Long (Book 5)

ABOUT THE AUTHOR

USA Today Bestselling Author, Renee George writes paranormal mysteries and romances because she loves all things whodunit, Otherworldly, and weird. Also, she wishes her pittie, the adorable Kona, and her corgi mix, Velma, could talk. Or at least be more like Scooby-Doo and help her unmask villains at the haunted house up the street.

When she's not writing about mystery-solving werecougars or the adventures of a hapless psychic living among shapeshifters, she dons her superhero cape and rescues kittens. Okay, so Simon and Ash just showed up and coerced her into adopting them.

She lives in Missouri with her family and spends her non-writing time doing really cool stuff...like watching TV, making pottery, and cleaning up dog poop.

Follow Renee!

Bookbub

Renee's Rebel Readers FB Group

Newsletter

www.ingramcontent.com/pod-product-compliance
Lightning Source LLC
LaVergne TN
LVHW010058110826
845155LV00028B/391

* 9 7 8 1 9 4 7 1 7 7 5 6 7 *